THOSE OTHER TIMES

THOSE OTHER TIMES

Bess Ross

Birlinn

This edition published in 2001by
Birlinn Limited
West Newington House
10 Newington Road
Edinburgh
EH9 1QS

www.birlinn.co.uk

First published in 1991 by Balnanin Books, Nairn

ISBN 1 84158 059 7

British Library Cataloguing-in-Publication Data
A catalogue record for this book is available
from the British Library

Printed and bound by
Omnia Books Ltd, Glasgow

for Tricia, Richard and Lucy

O N E

The Rent Man came early that day. Cis Clark sat at her kitchen table and put her fingers into her ears. From the room upstairs the sound of men's voices floated down to her. Seated as she was, the words were indistinguishable, just a rumbling mass of sound which rolled over and above her. She knew, however, their content, and that she could not hide from.

"There's two months owing." The Rent Man sat on the chair beside the bed and looked at John Clark.

John Clark said nothing. He tried to strangle the cough that he felt rising in him. His long boney hands lay to each side of him on the bed cover and he had about him that caved in look that illness and hardship bring.

"I knew nothing of this." His voice was ragged, his eyes dull. "I thought we were managing." And again he pressed his hand to the centre of his chest.

"Well, there it is," the Rent Man said, and he pushed

the book before him. "We've had nothing for two months."

"If it's there it'll be right enough," John Clark glanced at the book of figures. "But, as I've said, I knew nothing about it."

"I'm afraid you'll have to leave this house, Mr Clark. There's nothing I can do for you." And he put the book into a brown briefcase.

"Leave?" John Clark groped around inside himself for anything that would make some kind of sense to him. "How can we leave with five little bairns and another one coming?"

"I'm sorry, Mr Clark. There's nothing I can do for you." The Rent Man was on his feet. "If you can manage to clear up the arrears before the end of the month we would consider letting you stay on, but if not then you'll have to be out by the twenty-eighth. There are plenty waiting for these houses, you know." He walked to the door of the room, paused there a while.

"You're not in work at the moment," he accused from his closed face.

"I've been laid up for the past week," John Clark said. "It's the bronchitis again, do you see. And I've had a touch of the pneumonia." The colour had gone from his face.

"Yes, well, as I've said, the twenty-eighth." And he closed the door behind him.

He should stay in bed until the doctor came but he couldn't do it. Not now. Not with this about him. He'd thought they were getting on their feet at last.

He struggled from his bed and walked over to the wardrobe. Reaching into it he took from it his trousers and pulled them on, looping the braces over his shoulders. Then he brought his boots and stockings over to the bed and sat down on it to regain his breath, his hands spread on his knees. That was it then, he thought, and he bent to put his stockings on. What in God's name now? He tightened the lace of his boot. When he came back home after the war was done he never thought that things would be this way. Of course a man took whatever he could get in these parts. But that didn't worry him; he could turn his hand to anything. If he brought a wife with him it was harder. You told her what your home was like. It was a grand place, you'd find work no bother, you wouldn't be stuck. Then the bairns started coming and things weren't so easy, but still you managed. There was always the boat. The boat was good to you, it augmented whatever you made elsewhere. There was plenty fish in it.

Cis' legs felt like lumps of lead as she climbed the stair. So much was running through her mind that no coherent thought would form. The cough coming from the room was like a knife in her own chest. She felt for the knob on the door.

The drabness of that October day threw a grey veil over the room and its occupant. It contained only the most basic of furnishings, a double bed with a wooden chair to the side of it, and a black double wardrobe against the far wall. Grey mottled linoleum covered the floorboards and there was a grey bricked fireplace in the centre of the wardrobe wall. No fire burned in its hearth and no rug softened the floor.

John Clark was still on the edge of the bed, his long frame doubled to tie his other boot. Cis sat on the chair and tucked her feet beneath it. Her folded hands lay slack in her lap. Her eyes found her man's back, then looked past it to lock on the fireplace, as if it held for her something unknown and peculiar.

"What did he say?" she asked.

"You know what he said." And he went to the wardrobe. He took his black and white marled geansaidh from it, and pushed the door closed with the flat of his back. He pulled the jersey over his head. The room was silent. From beneath the chair, where the Rent Man had placed it, the clock ticked.

"When do we have to be out?" Her eyes were on the floor now.

"The end of the month. The twenty-eighth he said." And he leaned against the wardrobe as if somehow it would hold him upright.

"What are we going to do?" She twisted the wedding ring round her finger.

"I don't know what we're going to do. What can we do?"

"You're not going out?"

"I'm going to take a look at the boat."

"The doctor'll be here any minute. You can't go out."

"I'm going," he said and there was a hard edge to his words as he looked at her. Doctors! What good did doctors ever do him. What did they know about it anyway. Give up the sea, give up the fags, give up your life and be done with it. "I'll maybe take a walk overby later on. See if there's anything at all going there. Hugh would know." And he walked from the room.

"Try not to worry lass." He put his head round the door. "Something'll turn up." Then he was gone, his tacketty boots beating a tattoo on the bare stairs.

The front door closing roused Cis. She stood up and looked around the room. It was true they hadn't much and they didn't even get the bedrooms papered. But it was new and it was clean and it was theirs. Was.

Bending down, her hand reached for the clock and replaced it on the chair. Then she walked over to the window and opened it. She didn't look out. Out was grey, everything about this place was grey to her. A grey place with grey people. It wasn't like home, but then her mind conceded, what place ever was.

Her movements were slow and concentrated as she made the bed. She shook the pillows three times before she laid them in their place, she measured the distribution of the blankets on the bed as she pulled them straight, her fingers smoothed, caressed the textured reality of the heavy dark green cover.

After she had done that her inclination was to sit again but some force stopped her from doing that. She turned from the bed and walked from the room and back down the stairs.

Back in the kitchen she went to the sink and caught up the scouring cloth. She wiped the already clean cooker and was starting on the outside of the sink when the back door opened. A girl of about six years of age stood there. Her face and her jumper were dirty, and her fair hair came in a tangled mass to her shoulders. Green eyes challenged the world and her mother.

"I'm wanting a piece Ma. Can I get a piece and jam?"

Cis threw the cloth on the table and quickly crossed to the girl. She grabbed her by the shoulders and rattled her head on her young neck, so that her teeth banged together.

"Don't you ever forget," she cried to the ragdoll girl, "don't you ever forget that you have the best father in the world!"

The storm died within her as quickly as it had blown up. She reached for a kitchen chair and sat there.

"Can I get a piece Ma?" The child still stood in the doorway and eyed her mother.

"There's no jam." Cis reached for the loaf and the breadknife. She sawed a thick slice from the loaf and spread it with margarine. "Do you want sugar?"

"Ay," the girl had moved to the table, "I love sugar."

Cis took a handful from the brown paper bag and scattered it over the bread.

"I always love sugar," the girl said, and her mother handed her the slice. Then she drew the knife across her apron and replaced it on the overflowing table.

"You can go out and eat that," her mother said. "I want you to keep an eye on Dan."

"He's climbing on the pit again. He always cries when I try to make him come down." Her eyes knew contentment and her mouth was crystal.

"Go out and watch him for me," Cis said and the girl obeyed.

Cis twisted her hands together. She shouldn't have shook the bairn like that. She hadn't done anything. She picked up the cloth again and took it over the front of the sink.

From the window above the sink Cis watched her youngest. Alone in her world, Marjie was cramming the bread into her mouth as fast as she could. Little Dan was a soldier. His short legs carried him upright to about halfway up the side of the potato pit. Then, from where the slope inclined more steeply, he'd drop onto his hands and finish his march at a crawl. Once he reached his summit he'd stand upright once more and perform his conqueror's dance, his small boots stamping the ground beneath him and clapping his hands at his own cleverness. His golden head and child's laughter bathed the dullness of that place and was for a moment balm to his mother's heart. They'd be all right out there for a while.

Cis' thoughts drifted from her children and became concentrated once more. Her eyes took on a far seeing look and children and garden sped from her. Amid little Dan's laughter and Marjie's occasional shout she became aware of the gurgling sounds coming from the boiler. She'd miss the boiler. She'd miss it for the nappies and the towels and the sheets.

Getting this house had been a deliverance, for her at any rate. When the new council houses were being allocated she was sure they would get one. They had more points than anyone else whose name was on the list, the size of her family saw to that. And she had been right, as she was in so many things.

Their house in Hilltown had been very poor. A half-house in fact, its walls were crumbling and the damp was everywhere. A living room in which they slept, ate and cooked on the open fire and the closet for the bairns. And in the wet weather when everything had to be dried inside it was truly miserable. When she was handed the key to number four she thought she was a queen. She could do something for her family then.

Three bedrooms, a cooker and a boiler, running water. And the bathroom. She had forgotten what it was like to feel really clean, to feel fresh when she needed to feel fresh. And the electric light in every room. Everywhere so bright just by pressing a switch. She bought the electric iron. John was taking home regular money then and the extra he made from the boat got the marigold curtains for the downstairs room. In the summer her house looked beautiful, as the marigolds John planted beneath the big window rose to greet the golden curtains. She was the first in the row to put up lace curtains and then the others followed. John didn't care much for the lace curtains but she liked them. They had them at home. John thought they were specifically designed for people to peep through without others seeing them. Debtors Row they called the rows of windows in England. The women would lock their doors and peep through them at the tallyman.

Ay, she came from England. From the North East, harsh and gritty, with its people the same. But there was colour there, there was laughter, and the people, the men especially, worked as hard as anybody she knew; they cursed harder than anyone she knew, but they knew how to have their fun. Nobody seemed to know what laughing was for up here. She thought that she'd taken a step up for herself and now where was she to go. Back to what she came from. A rotten half-house in Hilltown, for that's all they could afford. Well, she wouldn't do it, she couldn't do it. Not that.

Cis took the piece of wood from the window ledge and,

lifting the lid of the boiler, she stirred the clothes in there. She let the lid drop and returned the stick which John had fashioned for her from the broken shaft of a hammer. Of course she'd go back. Where else would she go. Back was the only place for people like them. She'd go back to the filth she had stepped from, back to lifting every drop of water from the well and her guts torn from her through having bairns one after the other. Back to try and make good food for them from little and cooking it on the fire so that she had to fight the heat and the soot. And what if there was no fire and the bairns with gaping mouths? What then? She'd miss the cooker.

She took the cloth from the sink and wiped the front of it. Her heavy hair was still golden. With the back of her hand she brushed it from her forehead. The bairn in her was growing and was getting in the way of her bending.

It wouldn't bother John to go back, not the place anyway. It was his home, where all his family still lived. He was a Hilltown man and a Hilltown man never settled in Balmore. She was learning that fast. The villages stood back to back but you'd think John had moved to London to hear him. In fact he was more at home in England. He used to say to her he could settle anywhere, and he did during his years in the Navy. Ay, she thought, anywhere but Balmore. "It's no use, Cis," he'd say. "A Hilltown man's a Hilltown man and that's all that's to it." She'd never understand the ways of them up here. But there was more to it than that for Cis, and she acknowledged this. It was never far from her. His brothers and his sisters were alright in their way. Except his brother Earl. Whoever heard of such a name, of course it wasn't his proper name. He was an ignorant man who didn't know the first thing about how to treat people. But he didn't matter. It was his mother. She would never forget the reception she got from that one when she came here first. If her own mother only knew the half of it. No, she didn't relish going back near that one.

Little Dan's scream broke the air and chilled his mother's blood. From her kitchen window Cis looked at the pair of them on top of the pit. Little Dan's mouth swallowed his face and Marjie was stooped over him, her back an old woman's, her left hand darting off the side of the little fellow's face.

"The little witch." Cis' mouth tightened. "She couldn't keep her hands off that bairn." She'd soon teach her.

"Marjie!" She flung the door wide, her voice could be heard in the next village. "Marjie, if I catch you at that bairn again I'll tan your backside."

T W O

There were twelve houses in the block. Part of the government's rebuilding programme after the war, the planners chose Balmore, the largest of the three villages for their scheme.

Built of dark wood to a Swedish design they encircled a piece of waste land on which in olden times a monastery stood.

In these times the shows came and parked there, and dogs fought and did other things and boys, and sometimes girls, played football. The planners called the block Abbot's Crescent. To the locals and their neighbours they were the Swedish Houses. Eight of the houses were occupied by Balmore families, the remaining four went to Hilltown people. The Clarks were one of the Hilltown families and opposite them the Barclays were another.

Kathleen Barclay was Marjie's age and like Marjie she too was fair haired. There the similarity ended however, for where Marjie always had the appearance of some groundy thing that grew from the earth, Kathleen always looked brand new. Her hair fell in a shimmering curtain to the middle of her back, the pleats of her kilt were so sharp they were dangerous and her mother knitted her beautiful jumpers. For all that, however, she was but a shade only of the quick little girl on whose doorstep she sat. For where Marjie's face didn't know how not to smile, Kathleen's didn't know how to. Smiling might mean forgetting and forgetting could very well mean that she would end up just a small bit dirty. An only child, Kathleen was impressed by Marjie's huge bravado and by the number of children that lived in her house.

"Did you get anything?" She scrambled to her feet as Marjie came through the door with the usual shouting about her ears. Noise always came from Marjie's house.

"No," someone slammed the door at Marjie's back. "She says she hasn't got any," and she began to gnaw at the cuff of her already ragged jumper. "She has money, Kathleen. I saw lots of pennies in her purse."

Kathleen was quiet on that score. Her father gave her half a crown from his pay packet and her granny was forever giving her sixpence. She stood on the outer rims of her shiny shoes, but then she caught herself and put her feet flat once more.

"Coming to burn the brackens?" Marjie's green eyes threw the challenge to the grey ones looking at her.

"Where will we get the matches?" Kathleen's tone was adenoidal. There was also a measure of fear in the sharp intake of her breath.

"I'll get them. No bother." Marjie was brave. "Joyce'll give you matches for nothing. She'll give you anything for nothing. I just say they're for my mother and to mark them and she'll give them."

"I don't know, Marjie," Kathleen said, whose knowledge of such things hadn't even been born. Her small body seemed to move in sections, knees jerking here, elbows pushing in there, the ribbon on top of her head rotated like a helicopter blade. Burning brackens meant dirty and Kathleen wasn't allowed. Dirty would never bother Marjie, clean might.

"Are you scared?" she asked Kathleen.

"Well," Kathleen hesitated, "I'm not scared but I'm not asking for the matches. Don't make me, Marjie."

"I'll ask. I'll ask no bother," and there was sparkling devilment in the green eyes.

They had to turn left at the end of the crescent to reach Joyce's shop and there they met Billy and his old dog, Billy Vass. It looked like it had been many days since either had seen water and there was about both the same air of neglect. This in no way, however, dampened their joy of living. That day Billy Vass was taking Billy for his usual run.

"Fine day, fine day, fine day." Billy's face split in two when he saw the girls, while Billy Vass in his jerkiness and strength nearly had him off his feet. A cross between a collie and an alsatian at least, there was a lot of strength in him. Billy wound the piece of binder twine, which was Billy Vass's lead, another time around his hand. Kathleen held back behind Marjie lest any dirt from Billy or his dog might reach her, and flattened her back against the gable end of a wifey's house. Her hands went to smooth the perfect smoothness of her kilt and her legs twisted themselves around one another.

"We're going to burn the brackens, Billy," Marjie confided, as the rain came back.

"Yes, yes," said Billy. "Fine day." He had lost again in his struggle with his dog and his last words floated over his shoulder behind him as he bolted with it, his large colourful trousers and jacket billowing upwards and out, here and everywhere.

The light was on in the shop as it always was no matter what the time of day. It was a dark shop. Whatever light might have entered by way of the two small windows was kept very firmly out as Joyce stacked every imaginable thing there to display to her customers. The Typhoo Tea showed no concern beside the Knight's Castille Soap and tins of Zebo paid no heed to the baking soda invading their space.

Joyce was cutting bacon for a woman when they entered. Kathleen hung back, nervous by the door. Marjie walked straight to the counter and glued her eyes to the jars of black sugar sticks and rhubarb rocks and lucky tatties on the shelf behind. As always she tried not to look at Joyce's leg. She lost the battle and looked at Joyce's leg when she bent to scoop sugar from the bag for the woman. A small round woman in a flowered apron and with her hair in a neat bun, Joyce wore a strange black boot on one foot and rocked when she walked. Marjie was fascinated by the contraption, but at the same time a little afraid of what her mind was telling her. For Joyce's boot reached to her calf and something protruded from it there, under the leather. Her brother Duncan who was seven said that Joyce had two feet growing from the one leg in there and Marjie's mind added to it and found extra toes and wondered if the foot had bones like a real foot.

"Right, girls, what can I get you?" Marjie jumped when Joyce spoke to her. She wasn't feeling so brave about the matches now. The woman had finished and was making for the door. Kathleen almost dislodged the candles on the shelf at her back in her hurry to move away from her as she passed.

Marjie took a deep breath. "My mother's wanting a box of matches and mark it," the words rolled from her, loud in their innocence.

"Are you sure?" Joyce asked, her elbows on the counter.

"Sure as death." Marjie found the lucky tatties once more. She was half thinking of asking for one of them also but decided against it. She knew better than to chance her luck.

"Well, if you're sure," Joyce said, and her hand reached beneath the counter for the matches. "But mind," as Marjie's hand shot out like an uncoiled spring to snatch the small blue box, "I'm wanting a note the next time. You'll mind that now."

"Ay," said Marjie, forgetting to say thank you in her hurry to be out of the shop, in case Joyce should change her mind or guess what she was at. "Hurry, Kathleen," she hissed to her friend as she fled.

"What have you got there?" her brother Duncan asked, turning from the Zebo and baking soda and elbowing Kathleen to the side.

"Nothing," flashed Marjie and her hand reached into her wellington boot.

"You have so." He was still covered in freckles. "You put something in your boot. I saw you."

"I never did. I never did. I'm telling on you," Marjie spat.

"Tell me," Duncan threatened, "or I'll twist your arm."

"I never got anything. You can ask Kathleen if you're so smart."

Kathleen nearly fainted at their feet at this twist. "Kathleen'll tell you," Marjie was saying.

Kathleen remained mute and backed further away from Marjie's brother. He looked wild.

Duncan tried another tack. "Was it matches?" he asked. Marjie's look of astonishment told him he was right. "Did you mark them?"

"Ay."

"Give me some or I'm telling."

Marjie was beat. She tipped half of the box of matches into his outstretched palm. "Promise you'll not tell."

"Promise." His tone was careless as he judged the number of matches in his hand.

"Say honest," Marjie asked.

"Honest."

"Say honest to God."

"Honest to God, honest to God." He looked up from the matches. "Honest to God, honest to God, honest to God," and he put her matches into his jerkin pocket. "What are you going to do with them anyway?" he questioned both.

"Me and Kathleen's going to burn the brackens, aren't we Kathleen?" Marjie turned to Kathleen who wished she was home with her mother.

"I don't know," Kathleen said, and looked back to her shoes.

"I have fags," Duncan said, and took three crumpled cigarettes from his trouser pocket.

"That's Da's fags," Marjie's mouth was wide.

"I know. I got them in his tin."

"I'm telling on you Duncan Clark." Marjie's face narrowed, her eyes were slits.

"Then I'll tell on you," Duncan said.

Marjie thought about that one. "I'll not tell," she said.

"I'm going to sail them in a pool," Duncan said. "The matches can be the masts. Are you coming to do that, then we can burn the brackens."

"Ay, alright." That light was in Marjie's eyes. "Will we Kathleen?"

"I don't know, Marjie. I might get wet."

"You'll no get wet." Duncan inched nearer to her. "You can just watch."

"I don't know," she spoke to him from her chest, her eyes anywhere but at him.

"Well, I don't care anyway," Duncan said and booted a stone in the direction of Joyce's house opposite. "I'm off to the shore." And he turned his back on them, his hand in his pocket, clutching the crushed cigarettes.

The brackens covered a fair area of waste land that spread away from the back of the council houses. For the child who did not make the shore their second home the brackens was a good place to be. Marjie was at home in either place. The boys made their hideouts, or 'hutties' there and the girls made their houses. If Marjie was asked where she'd rather play she'd say the shore every time. The shore brought a risk however that the brackens never did and it wasn't only the sea. It was the weight of her mother's hand if she found out that she had been

anywhere near the place. So sometimes Marjie played
what to her mind was safe.

They walked up Joyce's vennel and this took them to
the field where the men played football. Through the
field and they were at the sloping russet bank. It was still
raining.

"Are you going to live in Hilltown?" Kathleen asked
the leader as they bored through the wet growth.

"Ay," Marjie answered. "I used to live in Hilltown."

"So did I too," Kathleen said, and they stood for a
while and smiled to one another.

Not going to the shore didn't save Kathleen. By the
time they came on some big girl's housie she was
wringing wet and the shine had gone from her shoes.

"That's a good whole cup," Marjie pounced on the
small pile of cups and plates in the corner of the house.
She picked it up, cradled it between her hands, felt its
china delicacy, studied its rosy pattern. "It has a handle
on. I'm taking this cup home."

Her mother didn't have cups like this. She had some
cups, but mostly they were chipped and their handles
didn't last long. She broke one herself in the morning.
She had it in her hand, then it was in pieces on the floor.
Just like that. She didn't know how it happened, it must
have been when she was thinking. Her mother gave her
a row, but that didn't bother her. She was always getting
rows. She was sad though when her father sighed.
Someone else would have to wait for their tea now. And
so she was taking this beautiful cup, likely the most
beautiful thing she had ever seen, home to her mother.
It would make her mother happy with Marjie this time.
Her face would go soft and she'd smile at her and praise
her.

"You can take a plate for your mother if you like," she said to Kathleen. "That one's whole as anything." And she made a crumpled face at a crumpled face china dog.

"My mother has plates," Kathleen said. "You better leave that things, Marjie. Someone might see us." But her face was more worried at the state of her shoes.

"Are you not even taking anything?" Marjie was getting tired of Kathleen. She never took anything wherever they were.

"I'm wanting to go home now. I think I'm wanting to go home."

"What about burning the brackens?" Marjie still held the cup. "Will we burn them now?"

"I don't know Marjie. I'm wanting to go home."

Marjie laid the cup carefully among the plates, then took the box of matches from her boot. Kathleen paled. Her tongue protruded from the side of her mouth as Marjie gripped the match tightly then struck it on the abrasive on the box. The flame rose, she bent over it to shield it and bore it to a bracken leaf. The flame kissed the wet growth, and died at once. She tried a second match. The same thing happened. She went on her knees and struck every match. There was a small pile of spent matches on the ground before her. Marjie was puzzled. Kathleen knew relief.

"If we had paper and paraffin I bet you I could've got them going." Marjie never knew when she was beat.

"Will we go home now?" Kathleen stamped the ground like a frisky foal.

"Ay," Marjie said, and retrieved her cup.

Kathleen led the way out, contriving somehow not to come into contact with any wet thing.

"If you want to you can come to my house and Mam'll give you supper," Kathleen said as they walked back through the men's field.

"Are you getting a good supper?" Marjie's hand was beneath her jumper holding tightly to the cup.

"We're having mince and jelly."

Marjie was dubious. Mince and jelly sounded good and her belly was gnawing at her. She swallowed, the taste of the mince already in her mouth. But jelly? She knew jelly, she saw the picture of it on the packets in Joyce's shop. Jelly crystals the words spelt. She could read that because Joyce told her what they were one day when she was studying the pyramid of boxes. But jelly belonged to another place altogether, one which she was too young to define. All that she did know was that she didn't expect to see jelly in their house. So, there was the jelly. But there was also some other thing which made her hesitate despite her desperate need for this ambrosia. And that other thing, up the front of her jumper, created an almost intolerable amount of excitement in her young breast.

"What about the cup?" Her eyes were large as she looked at Kathleen.

Kathleen rolled hers. Things always had to be complicated when she was with Marjie. Nobody else took other people's cups.

"You can leave it outside my house," Kathleen said.

"What if someone takes it?" There was urgent concern in her voice.

"Nobody'll take it." Kathleen was carefree.

"Someone might. Someone might just see it and take it."

"It'll be all right," Kathleen tried to soothe her.

In the discussion the cup had a near miss as Marjie, not looking where she was walking, collided with Joyce's gable end as they came back through her vennel. Marjie tasted fear then and her heart tried to escape from her chest. From then until she reached Kathleen's house she walked very slowly and with great care. It took her until then to be right again.

"Leave it there," Kathleen said as they stood outside her back door. Marjie searched around then bent to place the cup behind the pail for the ashes. As she walked behind Kathleen into her house she left her mind beside it.

"Can Marjie get supper with us, Mam?" Kathleen was bright in her own home. She went to her mother who was stirring something on a pan on the cooker and reached her arms around her and her mother bent and kissed her on the head. Marjie thought about her cup and wondered if the jelly was in the pan on the cooker.

"Would Marjie like that?" Kathleen's mother's tongue was different, but not like her own mother's was different.

Marjie was quiet in the order of Kathleen's house. Her eyes wandered to the table in the centre of the kitchen. There were silver forks and knives and spoons and a blue flowered plastic tablecloth, and glass tumblers. The only table that was in her house was crammed with all the things they ate, the sugar and the loaf and the jam. On a shelf high up on a wall were hundreds of pans, shiny pans. Maybe Kathleen's mother made an awful lot of jelly. Hanging by hooks from the shelf were cups. Kathleen's mother had lots of cups, thick blue ones and a pink one like her mother had, except Kathleen's mother's cups had handles. There were plain white ones of another shape and two thin, light cups sort of like her one beside the ash pail. Marjie's mother didn't have a shelf like that with cups on it. All their cups were on the table.

"Do you like jelly, Marjie?" Kathleen's mother turned from the pan to smile at her.

"Ay," Marjie said, turning from her cup counting.

"Jump up to the table then. This lot's ready. We'll not wait for Dad."

Marjie stared at Kathleen's mother, uncomprehending. She never jumped up or did anything else to a table. Except maybe to poke her rhubarb in the sugar bag when her mother wasn't about. They took their food anywhere there was a chair without someone on it. If there wasn't one empty they just stood. It didn't take long. The first one's plates were cleaned before their mother fed the last one. Her father said the lot of them could put the foulachs to shame. She didn't know why he said that.

The number of chairs around the table confused her. There were four and a big huge one. What if she sat on the wrong one, on somebody else's? She put her finger to her mouth and looked again at Kathleen's mother, then to Kathleen. She didn't know.

"There you are, Marjie." Kathleen's mother saved her by placing a plateful of mince and two potatoes in one of the set places. "Jump up now." She walked to the table and sat down on a chair. Kathleen giggled to her from her place. Marjie looked down at her plate and at the cutlery spread for her. Confusion came back. What way would she eat. She didn't know which hand to lift the knife with. She only ate with a fork in her house, or a spoon if someone else had the forks. Also she used her left hand to do things but in the intensity of that moment she forgot which hand that was. She looked first at one hand then to the other. She didn't know. She put her fingers to her mouth. Kathleen saved her when she lifted her fork and mashed her potatoes into her mince. Then she was right and her left hand went out to grip the fork without her even knowing it was doing it. Kathleen giggled to her again and Marjie laughed too loud and dropped her head again. She began by gobbling her food but a surreptitious glance at Kathleen's plate told her that it was still nearly full so with every ounce of what she had in her she made herself eat slowly, taking only the same amount as Kathleen on to her fork. Self consciousness kept her quiet and her head wedged firmly down.

She wasn't prepared for the form of the jelly. When Kathleen's mother placed it in front of her she stared at what was in the plate. She didn't know that jelly would look like that. She didn't know, either, what it would taste like but taste never crossed Marjie's mind. If it was edible she'd eat it, and even if it wasn't that wouldn't deter her.

She looked at the wobbly mass and her natural way of eating came back on her. She reached for the spoon and dug it into the jelly, trying to manoeuvre the complete lump to her mouth. Her chin hovered above the plate, the jelly was nearly in her mouth when the whole helping slid from her spoon, splattered her coldly on the knees and finished beneath the table, lying there like a breathing thing.

Marjie wanted to go home. Her reaction was to howl right there in Kathleen's mother's kitchen. She looked at the jelly. It looked huge. She didn't know how it ever fitted into her plate.

"Marjie fell her jelly, Mam," Kathleen was at her giggling again. Marjie felt hot, and tight, and she did not know what else.

Again Kathleen's mother sorted things for her. "That's alright, hen," and she scooped the jelly from the floor then wiped it with her cloth. "There you are now." and she placed an even larger helping in another plate and put it before Marjie. Then Kathleen tried the dodge and slowly let a small amount slide from her spoon. Her mother, however, would have none of it.

"You did that on purpose," she said. "Marjie dropped hers by accident." And Marjie felt a warm glow spreading through her.

"I better be going now," Marjie scrambled away from the table the moment the last spoonful was in her mouth. "Thank you for giving me my supper." She was in a hurry to be through the door. The food was past and her mind was back with the cup.

"Will you not stay for a wee whilie?" Kathleen's mother was at the sink. "Kathleen'd like that, wouldn't you darling?" she turned her head towards Kathleen.

"Yes, stay Marjie, stay," Kathleen begged, still spooning jelly.

"I have to go," Marjie said, and her legs wouldn't be still. "My mother'll be wondering."

"Alright. Ay, alright hen," and Kathleen's mother put her hands among the dishes once more. "Cheerio then."

"Cheerio," Marjie said. "Cheerio Kathleen."

"Cheerio Marjie," Kathleen giggled from the table.

She hung about until Kathleen's mother closed the door before she went for the cup. For a time Marjie thought that she would stand looking from her door all night. She pretended then to walk away, then bolted back at the slam of the door and the disappearance of the light which spread around her. She let go of her breath when the cup was back in her hands. It was still whole, nobody had touched it. She put it back under her jumper to protect it from the drizzle.

———————————————

They were all there when she went in. John Clark was in his chair in the living room, a last gripped between his knees. A small leather boot was on the last and he took a tacket from between his lips and hammered it into the heel. He took another, pressed it into the leather with his thumb, then he reached to his side for his small hammer and tapped the tacket home.

"Where were you?" His voice was easy, his eyes kind. "Your mother was beginning to wonder."

Marjie had got her mouth open but the words had not yet formed when Duncan, from the other chair, jumped in. "What about the matches? Tell about the matches, Da." He also smelt of rain.

"Never you mind matches." His look quietened Duncan. "That's for me to deal with."

"But she said she was going to burn the brackens." He couldn't hold his silence.

"Burn brackens! Burn brackens! And what was going to burn in this? Weather you wouldn't put an iron gate out in," and he spat a tacket into his hand.

"But she said."

"Now what did I say?" their father cautioned. "I said I would deal with this."

"What are you hiding up your jumper?" Grace came ben from the kitchen with a chunk of the loaf in her hand. She closed with Marjie and tried to find out.

"Get away, get away," Marjie's voice soared as Grace looked like winning the struggle. "That's Ma's cup," and the flood gates opened to wash a clean path down Marjie's dirty cheeks.

"Will the pair of you behave? Bagpipes now is it?" John Clark looked up from his cobbling. "Grace, leave the bairn alone. That'll do Marjie girl. You'd best go to your mother. Grace catch that little fellow. Look at what he's at," as little Dan examined the poker on the hearth.

Marjie stood in the open door which connected the living room and the kitchen and looked at her mother's back. She had the big black pan on the cooker and was tasting something from it.

"Are you making pudding, Ma?" The tears were forgotten.

"No, I'm not making pudding Ma." Cis didn't turn from the cooker.

"I love pudding." The grip she had on the handle of the cup was beginning to hurt her finger.

"Well, this is broth." Cis shook salt into the pan.

"I hate broth." Marjie shivered at its remembered taste. Her eyes watered.

"Well, you'll have to hate it then, because there's nowt

else." And she replaced the lid on the pan and walked to the table.

"I got you a cup, Ma," Marjie looked up into her mother's face as Cis sawed slices from the loaf.

Her heart looked from her eyes as she withdrew the cup from its safe place and handed it to her mother. She held her breath and she waited. However Marjie couldn't wait that long.

"It's a good cup, eh?" she said when it seemed that her mother would never speak.

Cis held the cup in her two work roughened hands. She cradled its shape, felt its fineness. With her forefinger she traced the pink roses growing around the rim. She held it to the light, saw the light through it. A film came on her eyes.

She was back in her mother's house. The smell of freshly baked bread intermingled with mansion polish filled her. She could hear her mother speaking. "Special china is for special people and that's what we are." Her mother never shut anything in a cabinet like some people did. If things got broke, then they got broke. She looked again at the roses and saw her father's garden. She pressed her fist beneath her left breast. The bread, the mansion polish and his roses, she'd smell them all her days.

"It's a good cup, eh?" Marjie's face showed her concern at her mother's strange silence. "I got it for you." Her eyes never moved from her mother's.

"Marjie, hinny, I think it's the loveliest cup I've ever seen," and she banished the dampness from her eyes with her warm smile. She held the cup to her breast.

"I could've got you plates too, Ma. I could easily have got you plates. There was hundreds of plates. All whole."

"No, no pet. Just the cup, just the cup," and her voice sounded strange to Marjie. She thought her mother would cry.

Cis put the cup on the table with the others and lifted the soup plates from it.

"Tell that lot that this is ready." She sounded like her mother again. "I don't know what you're going to have because there is nothing else."

THREE

They came back to Hilltown like covered waggoners of
the Old West, their possessions piled high on the salmon
fisher's trailer. Hilltown being Hilltown some charted
their progress from behind front curtains, but there were
those who came to their doorsteps and raised a hand in
greeting or waved the hem of an apron.

John Clark drove the tractor. Colin stood on the back
and bent over his father's shoulder and saw things
differently. Duncan and Grace, holding little Dan,
crouched at the back behind the chairs and watched the
road going fast. Cis put her good coat on and walked,
Marjie and Jeannie her companions on the way. Their
progress was slow and Cis, even though she felt burden-
ed with the weight of her child, managed to keep abreast.

"Are you alright there?" John Clark spoke to Colin.

"Ay."

"Are the others alright?"

Colin swivelled to look at the trio in the trailer. "Ay,
they're alright. They're just sitting."

They were quiet for a while.

"Will we soon be there?" Colin wished he could take
his hands from the mudguard and put them into his
pockets. His fingers felt numbed with the cold.

"Round the corner from the Post Office," his father
said. "It's not far."

They rolled past the row of houses with their smoke
reaching to the sky. As they came by the house with the
green window frames John Clark spoke again. "Look,

there's Dannac. I heard he was laid up."

"And there's my granny," Colin looked ahead.

John Clark lifted his hand from the wheel and returned the greeting of the frail, bent old man. "We'll
stop and have a word with your granny," he said.

Old Mrs Clark came from her doorstep into the middle
of the road and waited for them. "Will you come for a
cup of tea before you go east?" she asked Cis. "You're
looking tired maital."

"Hello, Mrs Clark," Cis said and stood straighter. "We
won't, thanks all the same."

"Are you sure, lassie?"

"I'm sure," Cis replied and looked behind her. "Jeannie, Marjie, come along."

Mrs Clark walked up to John Clark.

"Well, mother?" he said.

"That's you then," she said. "You won't stop?"

"No," he said. "We best be getting on. There's plenty
to do over."

"You're right," she acknowledged. "You know best.
God bless then." And she folded her hands across her
middle. "You'll watch you'll not fall from there," she said
to Colin and a hand reached into her apron pocket.
"Here, maital," and she handed him some pandrops.

"Thanks, Granny." Colin took the sweets, seeing only
kindness on her lined face. She had been a tall woman
when she was young and straight. Age had stooped her
some and taken the roundness from her. Her black skirt
reached nearly to her ankles and her jersey was rolled
many times to her elbows. "There, a sweetie for you,"
she walked to the back of the trailer. Eager hands

reached out and took the pandrops in silence, their eyes and their thoughts too shy to meet hers.

"We're going to our new house, Granny." Marjie was breathless from running everywhere. Jeannie was quiet at her back.

"You'll watch yourselves from that cars," their Granny said and reached into her pocket again.

"Ay. Cheerio Granny," Marjie said through a mouthful of pandrops. Jeannie said nothing as she savoured her minty spittle.

Mrs Clark walked back to John Clark. "That's it then. I'll send Hugh when he'll come," and she nodded to him, then to Cis.

"Yes, we best be moving," he said to her. "Are you bairns alright now?" and he twisted his neck to make sure.

The old lady stood in the middle of the road until the tractor and its followers went from her sight.

Their house in Bank Street was near the eastern end of the village. There were twenty four houses in the row. Their Granny's house was number twenty-four and their's was number three A.

Peg lived in number three B and Mrs MacIntyre lived with her man in number two. Three A was a half-house. There was a living room with an iron grate downstairs and a ben room, the closet. A tin scullery with a concrete floor had been added at some time. Up the steep, narrow stair there was only the one bedroom. The sloping roof ate into its space and a skylight let the light, or the dark in.

Marjie and Jeannie were the first up the path, their droopiness at the last stage of the journey vanishing at the sight of their house. "The door's locked," their father called as he climbed down from the tractor. "You'll have to wait," and he went to the trailer to rescue the imprisoned Grace, Duncan and little Dan.

"Mind, out of the way," Cis said to Marjie and Jeannie and she took the key from her coat pocket.

She stood in the centre of the living room and stared at its shabbiness. The noise of her children was all around her. Upstairs, someone was trying their best to come through the floorboards. She rested herself against the window ledge. The state of shock she'd been in since the Rent Man's visit fell away from her and she looked reality in the face. She looked at the peeling walls where someone had pinned a newspaper picture of 'Our Beloved Queen Mary'. She looked grimmer in her greyness. They'd never all fit in here.

"Are you coming to see the upstairs, Ma?" she heard Marjie before she saw her. "It's a good upstair." She stood in front of her mother.

"What am I going to do with him?" Grace was tired of humping little Dan on her hip and wanted to be off exploring.

"Keep him," Cis said and she walked to the lobby.

The small landing was fenced off by a piece of wire netting along the top of which ran a length of bamboo pole. Cis looked at it. "That'd be nice if you were a hen," she thought.

"Come on in here, Ma," Marjie was impatient.

Even in the middle of the day the landing was dark.

"Come on," Marjie's voice came to her.

It wasn't much of a room, but then it wasn't much of a house. She expected no more. Yellowing wallpaper covered in autumn leaves added to its dinginess. Someone had left a square of torn linoleum on the floor. Cis walked to the skylight to open it, automatically catching the cobwebs hanging from the iron frame and shaking them to the floor. When the cobwebs didn't move she took her hand down the side of her coat. "Come on, Marjie," she said and walked back to the stairs.

"Grace, I want you to go and ask your father if he took the paraffin. This is never going to go." Cis was on her knees before the grate. "The sticks are soaking."

"What'll I do with him?" Grace still had little Dan on her hip.

"Put him over there," and she nodded to a clear space. "Sit there pet," she spoke to little Dan. "Play with your car."

"There's a wifie at the door, Ma," Colin came in with the wireless.

"Well, who is it?" Cis got up from the floor with difficulty.

"I don't know. She just said were you in. Where will I put this?"

"Oh, put it where you like," her voice was ragged. "Tell her I'm coming. Not on top of my coat," she screeched as Colin placed the wireless there. "Put it against that wall."

"There's a mannie speaking to Da."

"Is there? I hope your father's not going to stand there all day."

Little Dan made unintelligible sounds from beneath Cis's feet and reached his short arms towards her. "I'll be back in a minute," his mother understood every sound. "Look, play with your car. I'm going to get the fire going and make something for us all," and she lifted the bairn and pressed her cheek to his soft one. "Stay here pet." She returned him to the floor.

Mrs MacIntyre was a big woman with short white hair which she kept in place with a kirby grip above each of her ears. Cis knew her by sight although she had never spoken to her. When they had lived in Hilltown previously their house was at the other end of the village.

"You have your sarachadh." There was kindness and understanding in the older woman's eyes. "Will you come for a drop tea? I have the kettle on."

Cis was about to refuse. She wasn't one for going into other people's houses. Then she thought of the dead fire and the bairns. "Yes," she said. "Yes, I will. Just as soon as I can get the fire going. This lot are going mad for food."

"Come now and never mind the fire. The fire'll wait. Come with the bairns."

"Yes, yes, alright. I'll just get my coat."

"I have the girdle on. We'll have a fresh scone," and her eyes were a young girl's. "Alec is giving a hand to John," she tossed her head in the direction of the gate. "They'll soon have things sorted. Just come when you're ready," and she went back down the path. Cis followed her a short way and collared Colin. "What about my paraffin? Did you ask your father?"

"I forgot," Colin said and struggled past with a wooden chair which he held before him. Duncan followed behind him with a cardboard box.

"Give me that." Cis lifted it from his hands. "Go back and tell your father I want the paraffin."

Cis doused the kindling and newspaper with the paraffin and sent flames flying up the chimney.

"It might go off." Grace moved away in her fear.

"No," her mother's voice discounted any such thing. "Your father thinks I can't light a fire," she confided. She placed the lumps of coal carefully on top. Little Dan began to cry again. "Ssh now, ssh now. It's alright pettie," Grace soothed and lifted him up.

"Where are the others?" Cis asked Grace.

"Colin and Duncan said they're not wanting to come. Jeannie and that Marjie are playing out the back."

"Right, that'll go," Cis said, and she put down the sheet of newspaper which she held before the bars.

"There's a dead hen in the barrel, Ma. It's white." Marjie found it hard to hold herself. "I can reach it with this stick. Look," and she stood on the tips of her toes and reached into the dark smelly water.

"I don't want to look," Cis said from the back step. "I'm too tired to look. Come away from that filth," and she walked past her.

"Where are you all going?" Marjie stood flat on the ground.

"To the woman next door. She's going to make us some tea."

"She was poking the hen, Ma. She was poking it all the time. She wouldn't stop," Jeannie's small tongue snaked from her mouth to feast on the snotters running from her nostrils. "She nearly lifted it. I'm frightened of the hen."

"Ha! She's even frightened of a hen. She's even frightened of a dead hen," there was derision in Marjie's voice.

"You can cut that out." Cis came back to stand behind Marjie. "Scaring the bairn," and her right hand tapped Marjie's cheek. "Now, do you want to come with us or do you want to stay?"

"What is she giving us?" Marjie asked as she trailed behind with Jeannie.

"Tea," Grace hissed and tightened her hold on little Dan.

They felt the heat and smelt the warmth of Mrs MacIntyre's kitchen as soon as she answered their knock.

"Sit you all down," Mrs MacIntyre said. "You take this chair, Mrs Clark," she said to Cis and she pointed to a large wooden chair with arms and a high back. "That one has a cushion," she said. "It'll be easier for you," and as an afterthought as she went back to her cooker. "Alec likes that chair. It's his favourite," she confided to them at the table. She put the lid on her teapot and placed it on the cooker. "We'll leave that brew for a whiley," and she buttered more scones. "Reach out your hands," she spoke to the children. "Don't be shy. I have more."

They didn't see their surroundings, shyness was forgotten as their hunger overcame them. Their eyes were rivetted to the heaped plate in the centre of Mrs MacIntyre's table.

"This is good scones," Marjie spoke through the first mouthful. "I love scones," and she did her best to finish what was left with the second bite. Grace looked at Marjie. Her eyes told her to stop her nonsense at the same time as her foot collided with Marjie's ankle. Little Dan's struggles were becoming too much for Grace, as his hand went out to grab everything.

"Give him here, Grace," Cis said, and she reached for him. "Take yourself a scone."

"That's you," Mrs MacIntyre's bore the pot to the table. "I have more. Help yourself, lassie," and she filled the cups. She handed Cis hers first. "I put plenty milk in for the bairns," she said.

"Thanks very much," Cis took the cup. "I'm dying for this," and she held little Dan away from her hand.

"Ach, it's nothing," Mrs MacIntyre waved her words away. "It's nothing at all. Just a cup of tea," and she walked round the table. "Drink up, maital," her hand smoothed Grace's dark head. She filled a cup for herself and sat down beside them. "Will he take some milk?" she asked Cis.

"Yes. Yes, that'd be grand, thank you."

Mrs MacIntyre came back to her chair and leaned her elbows on the tablecloth.

"They'll soon get things sorted," her mouth was kind as she spoke.

"Yes," said Cis, juggling between little Dan and the cups.

"You're looking tired. Did you walk?"

"Yes."

"Indeed, you're looking tired."

"I'm just a bit," Cis said.

"Once you get the lino laid it'll not take long. That big boys are a big help."

"Yes." Cis was proud.

"Once they get the lino laid they'll soon put the heavy things in. Alec'll not stop till it's all in."

"That's good," Cis said and sipped her tea. She was grateful for it, for the life it seemed to give back to her and the reason it gave her to stop awhile. The cushioned chair welcomed her and could have retained her for long enough. Her shoes felt tight on her feet. She knew her ankles were like balloons. The morning, when she rose from her bed, seemed to belong to another time. Balmore was past and there was Hilltown now.

"Look at him," Mrs MacIntyre smiled. "He's enjoying that," and she looked at Grace, Marjie and Jeannie. They looked up at her in silence, then went back to their eating.

"Your scones are lovely," Cis said.

"Ach, I just threw them together. Take another one."

"No. No thanks. I'm enjoying the tea."

"Ach well, you could be doing with it."

Cis drained her cup. "Are you lot finished yet? I'll have to be getting back."

"My tea's not done," Marjie tipped her head back and tried to slurp every grain of sugar from the bottom of her cup. Grace looked at her, her distaste at the habits of her sister spread across her face. If she took her finger round the bottom of the cup she'd kick her. Right there in the wifie's kitchen.

"You're finished," her mother said. "Come on."

Marjie rammed the rest of the third scone home.

"I'm finished," Jeannie said and she sniffed.

Mrs MacIntyre put two buttered scones into a brown paper bag and handed them to Marjie. "You'll take that to your father. And here," she spoke to Grace, "You'll take this," and she handed Grace an enamel mug of tea. "Watch yourself now. It's hot."

"Thanks," said Cis from the doorway. "I'd better see how they're managing."

"It was nothing," Mrs MacIntyre said and she went to take dishcloths from her washing line as they returned to their house.

———————————

John Clark and Alec MacIntyre smoked their cigarettes and took their breaths.

"That's it anyways, John." Alec MacIntyre blew smoke from his mouth.

John Clark took a long pull and looked at the house opposite. "Ay, that's it man."

The men were sitting on the dyke which ran along the bottom of his garden. "It took longer than I would have believed," John Clark said. "I'd have been stuck without you."

"You always have more than you think, John. The little fellows are done, I think."

"They worked hard," their father said. "They never stopped."

"Ah, well, they'll sleep the night John," Alec MacIntyre said.

They were quiet for a time, each thinking their own thoughts.

"Are you doing anything just now, John?" Alec MacIntyre broke their silence.

"Work, do you mean?" John Clark asked.

"Ay, are you at anything?"

"I was thinking to try for something when we're settled here. I'm going off the sick. To hell with that. Who can live on what you get from them," and he screwed the end of his cigarette on the dyke.

"I was thinking to go up to Bain's in the morning," Alec MacIntyre said. "They'll be needing someone for the clipper. I could ask for you."

"Ay, ay. That's good of you man. I'll not be able to shift till I'm finished here. I've one or two things to collect from overby yet. I think I'll leave that till the morning. I want to be clear of the place."

"Surely, man. Surely. I'll ask for you. I can easily ask."

"I'd be grateful," John Clark said, and his thanks looked from his eyes.

"I better go and see what herself's doing then," Alec MacIntyre put his cigarette end beneath his boot. "She'll kill me if I take this in with me," and he pressed down with his heel. "I'll be seeing you then, John."

"Ay, I'll be seeing you Alec."

The daylight was fading from the October sky. John Clark sat awhile as darkness crawled into his new beginning. The house opposite had its electric lights on and he could hear the noise of his children at his back. Cis would be having a right time with them. Duncan had at last climbed from the seat of the tractor as his empty belly overcame his fear that if Colin took the seat he'd never get a shot. Duncan was some lad, he thought. Colin worked like a man. He was a big strong fellow even although he was just past twelve. The battle which raged in number three sounded as if it was dying down. The only thing that ever closed their mouths was food. To-day, maybe it was tiredness. It had been a long day for them all and they were only little bairns.

The light cast by the naked light bulb hanging from the flaking ceiling did nothing to improve the room. Our Beloved Queen Mary looked tired. It could have been the weight from her crown or maybe she had just been on the wall too long. The damp stain on the far wall, against which they had pushed the big bed, seemed to have spread itself with the light and had taken the appearance of some hulking beast. Cis was at the grate, stirring up the contents of the big black pan. She was battling against the blowback from the fire, which filled her hair and her mouth and took the tears to her eyes.

"This is no use," she spoke to the row on the settee beneath the window. "I can do nothing with this," and another black cloud came at her. "What am I meant to do with it?" her eyes besought theirs. They looked back at their mother and said nothing.

They were quiet at last, every last ounce of their energy was spent. The weariness of the day dulled their eyes.

"Get yourselves a plate then," their mother said.

Duncan was the first in line. "It's porridge," he said, finding from somewhere the heart to protest.

"I know it's porridge," his mother said. "It's all there is," and she spooned the clotted mass into his plate. "And you needn't look like that," as he twisted his mouth out of its shape.

Marjie was more enthusiastic. "I love porridge," she said and nearly dropped the lot in her hurry to be sitting and eating.

There was no problem with Jeannie. She took her plate and sniffed. Colin was starving. He was growing fast. Grace refused. "I'm not eating that," she said.

Cis hadn't the fooshion to argue with her. "Want then," she said. And as John Clark came in, "Hurry up someone. I need a plate for your father."

"I'm not hungry," he said and sat on the wooden chair beside the door. "See to the bairns first," and he took a slim cigarette from his tobacco tin.

Cis took little Dan on to her lap and sat in the armchair by the fire, a plate of milky porridge at her elbow. She held little Dan tightly and tried to tempt his mouth to open with the first spoonful. Little Dan was too tired and didn't know what way he was meant to be. He took his small fist and knocked the spoon away, scattering its contents on to his mother's apron. Then he lifted his clarty hand to his ear and rubbed porridge into it, and into his hair. Cis scraped the mess from her front and put the plate and the spoon on the table. "You're dead beat, my little lamb," she said and folded his baby body against her breast. At the soothing sounds, rocking movements and the warmth from his mother his heightened rigidity gave way to a drowsy fluidity, and in what seemed like no time at all he lay asleep against her. She gave him a while and when she was certain that his sleep was deep she lifted him to the big bed and put him beneath the blankets.

"I've told you about that fags," she said to John Clark as he started coughing. "You'll have the bairn awake, you will." She went back to her chair. "Do you want anything to eat?"

"No," he nearly strangled himself. "I'll take a cup of tea when you're making it," and the cough doubled him in two. When the spasm had spent itself he looked across to the occupants of the settee. Their small fresh faces and young eyes carried a worry that was beyond their years. He saw this worry.

"Hee ya, hoo ya, cheeshell, cheeshell," he pretended to cough his guts out again. They knew him and they laughed at his joking. Hearts knew relief, and as they turned and laughed too loud to one another eyes showed that relief.

"That fags'll kill you," Cis said to him and she spooned little Dan's porridge to her mouth.

"No nor kill," his tone was dismissive. "What's a fellow supposed to do? Hm?"

He hung low in his chair, his hand clutching the cigarette dangled between his knees. His gaze was fixed on the floor. It was good to get the lino from Hugh. It was lucky for them that the camp was in it. It wouldn't stay the colour of the sand long in here. The lavatory pan and the bath was no good to them. What were they going to do with them? That minded him. He'd have to put a pail out the back in the old henhouse. Maybe two. There was one or two things needed doing, that chimney would have to be cleaned before he started on anything else. He put his cigarette between his lips, he drew deeply.

"Is their beds made?" he looked across to Cis.

"Yes."

"Well, when you ones are done I think you should be going to your beds, like good bairns."

"Are we not getting our tea?" Duncan made slurping sounds from his spoon.

"There's no tea for you," his mother said. "You've had all the milk."

"Crivvens, no tea," his face appeared to crumple inwards.

"Yes, crivvens no tea," his mother said. "You can't get blood from a stone."

Duncan remained in his crumpled state. His mother was always saying that.

"Are we not getting ANY tea?" Marjie pursued.

"You heard," her mother's tone was short.

"Look, the lot of you, you heard what I said," their father said. "Up the stair now till your mother'll get a little peace. Think of the bairn," and he nodded towards little Dan.

"Have I got to go with them?" Colin asked.

"Like a good fellow," his father said.

"Och, man, it's early yet," the tears weren't far from Colin. He'd worked hard all day and his father was treating him like a bairn.

"Never mind early," his father was upright in his chair.

"Up, I said."

They rose in mutiny.

"I'm doing my pee," the tiredness had robbed Jeannie's face of its colour.

"There's a dead hen in the barrel," Marjie remembered to tell. "It's white. You can poke it with a stick. You can poke its head."

"Will you just get yourselves off," their mother sat slumped in her chair, her left hand lay on the mound of her belly.

"I'm doing my pee too," Duncan said.

"They'd better not pee the bed," Grace sounded sullen as she looked at Jeannie and Marjie.

"If they do I'll tan their backsides," their mother said as she came from her chair.

John Clark turned to her as she walked past him. "Have you any kind of tin for them?" he asked, and she went into the closet.

"There," she brought out an enamel basin. "You can use that," and she handed it to Duncan.

"Do I have to go with them?" Colin tried again.

"Just for the night," his mother said. "You can go in the closet tomorrow night."

"We'll have it sorted for you tomorrow night," his father spoke to him. "Just go up for the night."

Duncan took the basin to the back kitchen. When he returned Jeannie and Marjie and Grace argued their way through. Grace came back first.

"Will you be coming up to see us?" Grace asked her father.

"I'll be up in a little while," her father said. "You go up like good bairns."

"I was wanting tea," Duncan said as he went through the door. Resignation made little old people of them. Their chins were on their chests as they climbed the stair.

"Watch yourselves," their father called after them.

"Do you want some tea without milk?" Cis asked her man.

"That'll do fine. A drink is all I want."

He came from his chair and crossed to the fire. From the pail beside the fender he took some blocks of wood and added them to the embers. Cis lifted her blackened kettle and poured boiling water into the pot.

"A drink is all I want," John Clark said and sat down in the other arm chair. "That's good sticks," he said as they flared at once. He sat on the edge of his chair and reached a spread hand to their warmth and their life. Cis poured tea into his mug.

"I was talking to Alec," John Clark said as he sipped his tea. Cis swilled the porridge plates in the basin. She waited.

"He's going up to Bain's tomorrow," he said and flexed his fingers before the heat. Cis shook water from the spoons and placed them on the table beside the plates. "He said he would ask for me."

"That was kind of him," she wiped the plates with the dishcloth. "What about the sick?"

"I'm coming off the sick."

"You'll have to go in to them to sign off. The doctor won't come out you know."

"I'll go in. As soon as I get the rest of the stuff over."

"What work?" she dried the spoons as one.

"The clipper."

"The clipper," she stopped what she was at and looked

at him. "Clipping turnips! You can't go clipping turnips. That'll kill you, man."

"Well, kill me or no, if I can get a start I'll have to try," they looked at one another for a time. "I'll have to try," and he tipped his mug to his mouth.

"How many weeks will it be for?" Cis was back in her chair. She stretched her legs before the fire.

"It'll be two or three weeks anyways. I would say two or three at the least. I might get taken on for the tatties after that. That would be alright."

"That could take us up to Christmas."

"If he takes me on," he threw more wood onto the fire. "I'll clean the chimney in the morning," he said. "I'll go to Hugh for the brush."

"You'll have to do it early then. I can't be without a fire. We'll perish."

"I'll do it first thing. I'll go for the brush the night."

The new wood crackled behind the bars of the grate. Up the stair the babble had died completely.

"I was thinking if I got the start I could maybe distemper this place. The distemper would make a difference. Freshen it up for you."

"Hmhm, and the bairns are going to need something for their feet."

"The bairns'll get their boots, I'll guarantee that. Yes, the bairns'll get their boots wherever they come from."

"We'll not stop here long, will we?" and he looked at the fear that was in her eyes. He knew what she saw when she first walked through the door.

"No, we'll not be here long. Just as soon as I'm back on my feet I'll look for something else, a decent place."

"I don't think I'll be able to stand it here. Our new

house was lovely. It was a lovely house." In her tiredness she was no longer able to keep that memory back.

"Don't upset yourself like that," John Clark said. "It was a lovely house, a good house, but we'll get something else. Don't go upsetting yourself about it."

"If only we could have stayed."

"We couldn't stay so there's no use speaking."

"Where are we going to get anything. We haven't a halfpenny."

"We'll get something, don't you worry. There's bound to be a place somewhere."

"You wouldn't go back there, would you?"

"No, I'll not go back to Balmore. That place is not for me. But some place."

"Do you have to put the tractor back the night?" her face showed concern at his frailty. There wasn't a spare ounce of flesh on him.

"No, Sandy said tomorrow would do for them. I'll finish up overby after I do the chimney. Then I'll have to go in to sign off. I have still my fishing gear to get and the big wardrobe. I don't think that wardrobe'll come in here. It's big."

"It'll have to come in. Where am I going to put anything? All I've got is the dresser."

"I'll see anyway. I would need a hand though. Maybe Alec'll be about." He thought for a while. "What about the cupboard in the closet?"

"You can't put things in there. It's rotten with damp."

"Of course it could serve for my lines. It would always do for that."

"Well, it's fit for nothing else."

"Is the bottom of it not dry enough?"

"None of it's dry. Haven't you looked at it man? Look if you don't believe me. Although you'll smell it first."

"Anyways, it's a roof above our heads."

"Ay, and that's thatch covered in felt. The place'll be lousy."

He said nothing. There was nothing more to say.

"I never thought my life would turn out like this," Cis said. "You never do, do you, think what your life will be like years ahead?"

"How does anyone know what their life is going to be," he said. "No one knows that."

"You never think of the road you might take, do you? You're so sure of the road you're going to take."

"That's youth, lassie. Everyone thinks they're right when they're young."

She started humming. The notes from '*Veelia*' from *The Merry Widow* floated from her lips and went around the little room. She stopped and looked at him. "I used to go to the opera you know."

"I know," and his face softened towards her.

"Sometimes I'd go every week. As soon as I got my pay."

"I know that," he said.

"I loved the opera. Sometimes our Mary'd come but she liked going to the pictures better. But I always went."

"Yes," he said, and his eyes were on the floor.

"Do you remember when you first met me? I bet you can't," her tone was teasing.

"I always mind that," his voice was low, soft.

"I bet you can't tell me what I was wearing," she said.

"It was some kind of frock thing."

"Some kind of frock thing. Don't be daft. That suit I was wearing came from Harrods I'll have you know."

"Well, what do I know? It's only yourself I noticed," and his grin was wide.

"It took six months to pay that suit."

"Worth every penny I would say," the grin was still across his face.

"You can't even remember," and she lifted someone's sock from the fender and threw it at his mouth.

No, he thought as his hand caught the sock from the air, he didn't remember about frocks and things, but there was plenty he did remember. He reached for the poker and   put it between the bars to loosen the ash. And he was no different to any fellow who fell in love with the loveliest girl he'd ever seen. He was going to reach up to the stars and catch the brightest one that was in it and press it into her hand, then he would stand and wait for the magic words she would say to him.

He shook his head as if to clear something from it. His memories mocked at him as he lifted his head and looked at the place. Stars, was it? This here was the reality. The bairns up the stair without a drink of tea and a tin dish to piss in. Raised voices from above took Cis from her chair.

"You sit," he said. "I'll go up to them."

John Clark patted the blankets around Jeannie's shoulder and down behind her back. He moved to the bottom of the bed and did the same for Marjie. "Keep yourselves warm now," he said to them.

"Can I get on the seat of the tractor tomorrow, Da?" Duncan lay raised up on his elbow.

"We'll see. If you're a good boy," and he pulled the blankets about him. "Keep yourself warm now. Alright Col boy?" he spoke to the dark head protruding from the top of the bed. "That's it," he said in answer to Colin's indistinguishable sounds.

"Grace is putting her feet in my face all the time," Marjie's voice soared from her. "Ow, that's sore," as Grace kicked her for telling. Marjie drove her two feet into Grace's side.

"Is the pair of you going to cut that out. Can you not even sleep in peace?" he was stooped beneath the sloping ceiling.

"My feet's not even touching her," Grace said from the top of their bed.

"And her and Jeannie has all the blankets. I'm freezing here."

"We haven't all the blankets," Grace said and unleashed a foot again.

Jeannie said nothing. She was only little.

"Alright Jeannie sweetheart?" her father patted the blanket about her again. Jeannie coughed and he clapped the top of her head. She coughed again and snuggled against Grace's back and felt safe.

"Can you move your legs a wee bit Grace and give this one some room. That's a good girl."

"I can't breathe with her big legs," Marjie said. "I'm nearly crushed into the wall."

"Half a dozen could get in there," their father said. "Look at the room that's there," and he lifted the army coat from the floor and spread its weight evenly about them. "Now," he said. "Is that it for the night?" He stood in the centre of the room and spoke to the two beds. "Go to sleep now." He walked to the door and turned back on them. "And mind you all say your prayers."

"I said mine," Duncan said.

"I said mine," Jeannie's voice was small under the sleeve of the big coat.

"Well, mind, the rest of you," he said and went down the stair.

They settled then. Their father had put them right.

"That's them anyway," he said to Cis as he re-entered the living room.

"I don't like Colin up there. He's a big lad now," Cis said.

"It's only for the night," he said and he went back to his chair.

"Was that Jeannie I heard coughing?" Cis asked him.

"Yes, but she's alright."

"I don't like the cough that's on that bairn. She's always coughing," Cis said.

"She'll be right enough," he said. "It's quite warm up there. How's the bairn?" and he looked at the small mound in the centre of their bed.

"He's sound," she said. "Do you want any more of this tea?" and her hand lifted the pot from the top of the grate.

He handed her his mug.

"It's a bit strong," she said as the black liquid flowed from the spout.

"As long as it's wet," he said. "I'm going to put a light into that scullery," he said, "and one above the back door. So we'll see where it is we're going." He took a gulp from his mug. "Hugh has all the tools. He'll give me a hand," he took the lid from his tin and lifted out a cigarette paper and scattered some tobacco along it. Then he drew the paper between his lips and put one edge up and on to the other, and rolled the cigarette between his thumb and forefinger. He put it into his mouth. "You can't see a hand in front of you out there," he said. "We'll need a light for the pail," and he poked his cigarette between the bars and waited until it lit.

"I'm going to take this tea and then I'm going for the chimney brush," he said. "You should get yourself to your bed when they're at peace," he said. "There'll be enough to do tomorrow, if all's well."

F O U R

"Did he say how much he would pay for the acre?" John Clark asked Alec MacIntyre as they walked on the road to the farm.

"Four pounds and ten shillings for the swedes, he said. Two pounds and ten shillings for the yellows. They haven't much yellows," Alec MacIntyre replied.

The village lay below them as they travelled on the top road, its points of light breaking the darkness. The hard frost cut their breath from them as they walked, the tackets of their boots struck sparks from the surface of the road.

They huddled into their clothing, one man tall and spare, the other shorter, and round. Alec MacIntyre's face was a moon, his mouth and eyes smaller circles. Their bonnets were pulled well down on their heads, their jacket collars were pulled well up around their necks. Their piece bags were slung across them, the clipper blade showing from one corner.

The sound of voices floating on the clear, sharp air took them through the farm square and into the stable. The grieve and his horseman and the boy were standing there. The stable felt warm. Heat spread around them from the two horses in their stalls.

"Ay, man," John Clark spoke to the three men.

They looked towards him. "Ay, man," they all replied.

"Ay, ay," Alec MacIntyre said.

"Ay, ay," they all replied and the horseman lifted down a collar from a wooden peg on the wall, and walked over to the black horse. The boy rocked backwards and forth on the balls of his feet and looked at the floor. The grieve said, "It's as hard as hell out there," and smiled. They agreed that it was that alright and the boy laughed as if someone had said something funny. John Clark looked at his downbent straw head and wondered if the fellow was right. "It may soften," he said to the grieve.

"Ay, likely," the grieve said.

"Yes, indeed," Alec MacIntyre said.

The farm men had a secure, closed look about them. They had never known what it was to go looking for work. Theirs was always there for them.

The black horse was restive with the horseman at him. He spread his mood to the brown horse and the brown horse began backing against the sides of his stall and tossing his huge head. The horseman made soothing sounds from low in his throat into the ear of the black horse and the black horse settled.

"I doubt if we'll manage to do more than scratch the ground the day," the horseman spoke to his horse. "It's like iron out there, eh boy." He made clicking sounds from his tongue and the horse came for him, the men backing away from his size as he walked from the stable.

"You can make a start on the yellows," the grieve spoke to them. "They're in the short field. The yellows are two pounds and ten shillings the acre. There's not much of them. The swedes are four pounds and ten shillings the acre." He turned his head towards the boy. "You go with them, George."

"Ay, ay," the boy laughed to the grieve and lifted his hand and scratched the side of his head.

"Mind you'll go easy with the hook," the grieve said. "They're for the pit. I'm not wanting them damaged."

"Yes, yes," Alec MacIntyre said and led them outside. "Best get to it."

John Clark nodded his understanding to the grieve as he walked past him. The boy came at his heels with a shuffling walk.

The short field was long, but narrow.

"I don't know about you John," Alec MacIntyre said, "but I'm thinking we're going to be hard pushed to make our money in this," and he looped his bag over a fence post.

"I was reckoning we could do the acre in two to three days if the weather was right. We'll take the week the way it is just now."

"That's what myself was thinking," Alec MacIntyre said, his hand gripping his chin as he studied the field.

"Anyways, we're here," John Clark said and he took his clipping blade from his bag and stroked his thumb down its cutting edge.

The clipper was a sickle shaped implement. Its sharp blade sliced the roots and the shaws clean from the turnip. It had a hook at the top end of the blade which was used for hooking the turnip from the ground. However, in ware which was going to the pit, the hook was never used as broken turnips went bad. On these turnips the men had to use their hands only to tear the crop from the hardened earth.

John Clark and Alec MacIntyre took drills beside each other. The boy spoke no word and slipped and stumbled to the far side. They straddled their drill and bent their backs. They gripped the turnip shaws and tugged.

"The boogers are not wanting to come," Alec MacIntyre's belly was between his knees.

"Well, if they'll not come this way," John Clark said, "they can come another," and he used the toe of his boot to kick the turnip loose. When it wouldn't budge that way he tried gripping the shaws again. The shaws were like glass with the rain frozen on to them. The day hadn't even started and the hacks on his thumbs had opened with the cold. The harder he gripped, the sharper the pain in his hands. He straightened his back and took the back of his hand across his mouth. He bent his back again. He got the booger this time. He chopped off its top and its tail and threw it to the side.

"How're you doing, John," Alec MacIntyre spoke across to him. There was one bare, purple turnip lying beside his left boot.

"This is no blinking use. We'll make nothing from this," and he carried on. He could build up no rhythm, no way he could build up any heat. His feet were that cold they were speaking to him and his back was in two. By dinner time his hands would be in bits. He tried to take a stronger grip of the clipper handle but it was no use. His fingers were dead and would do nothing for him. Ahead of him he saw Alec. Alec seemed to be going better than him the day. The coughing burst from him and nearly put him onto his knees. He kept on. His trousers were soaking with the shaws and there was four turnips lying in his row. Over on the far side the boy was shouting. Alec MacIntyre and John Clark stopped at this and straightened themselves and looked. The boy was full stretch on the ground, wrestling with a big one. He pulled it this way, he tugged it that way, and the swears fell from his mouth. "Come out, you big bastard," they could hear him clearly, and he spread himself over the turnip the way a man would cover his wife.

"Are you looking at that?" Alec MacIntyre asked and John Clark shook his head. "I'm not thinking that fellow's right," he said.

John Clark took his watch from his trouser pocket and looked at it. He looked at his row of turnips behind him. There was nothing much there.

"It's five to," he called to Alec MacIntyre who was just ahead now. "We'd be as well to stop now for our half yoking."

Alec MacIntyre heard him. He turned his head. "You're right, John. I'm needing it."

"What about that fellow?" John Clark asked Alec MacIntyre when he had come to stand beside him. Alec MacIntyre looked across the field. "Ach, let him be," and they walked over to the fence.

"This is dirty work," Alec MacIntyre unscrewed the cup from his flask. "I'll tell you this, John, you work for your money. Look at that," and he spread his torn hand below John Clark's face.

"Oh, they expect their pound of flesh, Alec, I'll grant you that alright," John Clark put a cigarette between his lips. He leaned back against the fence and reached for his tea. "You know, Alec, I don't think we'll make anything out of this. It could take the whole week to make the acre. You could reckon to do two in the normal way."

"Oh, I don't know what to be saying to it," Alec MacIntyre said and took a bite from his wife's scone. "There's nine of them drills to the acre. We'll be lucky to do a half of one the day," Alec MacIntyre had worked the clipper on the farm every year. "Are you for a scone?" he asked and he stretched his piece box before John Clark. "She always makes too much."

"No, I'm fine man. I'm needing this," he said and looked at his cigarette.

"It could soften," Alec MacIntyre scattered scone crumbs from his mouth.

"Not when it's as hard as this. We'll be lucky to see any sign at all of the sun," John Clark lit a cigarette from the end of the other one. He smoked it then threw the tea from his cup. "Time for us to be some place else," he said and rose from the wet grass. Alec MacIntyre finished his wife's small cake and put his tin and flask into his bag. "I'm stiff to move once I sit," he said and rolled on to his knees before coming upright. He cast his eyes over what was waiting for them.

"The things are no even good for the soup," he said and his voice was filled with his disgust.

They worked on until dinner time and made very little headway. Nothing came from behind the cloud to soften the earth. The field, a grey umbrella spread over it, was the world. And if the pain from John Clark's thumbs nearly took the tears to his eyes, not even the seagulls knew about it. At the end of their first week there the grieve put three pounds, four shillings and eightpence into their hands. It took them to the end of the second week to free the yellows from the earth's iron fist.

―――――――――

"Is Da home yet?" Duncan asked as soon as he came into the house.

"No, he's not home yet," Cis prodded the potatoes in the big pan with a fork.

"When will he be coming?" Duncan was hovering about the table looking for something for his mouth.

"I've told you. He'll be home at supper time. Soon," she replaced the lid on the pan. Ever since their father started at the farm it was always the same question they asked. If she'd a sixpence for every answer she gave she'd be rich.

"When's it going to be supper time?" Duncan's hand reached out to the loaf.

"When your father comes," Cis was beside him. She brought the fork across the back of his hand. "Leave that bread," a growl came from her throat. His hand stopped what it was about to do and he gave a small leap.

"I'm flipping starving," he pushed forward his bottom lip.

"Starve," he gained no comfort from his mother.

"Where's the rest?" he asked.

"How should I know? Grace took the others to the well. Colin's somewhere." She gave a large sigh as she lowered herself back into her chair.

"What are you making in the pan?" Duncan still stood at the table. There was the chance yet that his mother would turn away or rise and go out to the back for something.

"Tatties," his mother said. "It's sleeshacks the night."

"I love sleeshacks," and a light shone from him as he looked at her.

"Ay, well, you'd have to," his mother said. "Get away from that table."

"How," his tone was querulous. "I'm not doing anything."

"You heard," his mother said.

"Crivvens," he said and lifted his foot to the table leg. "I'm going to meet Grace and them."

"Go," his mother called after him when he was going through the closet door. "Go and stay," she thought when he was from her sight.

Cis felt bad. This bairn she was carrying was different to the others. Of course every bairn was different to her, but there was more than different about this one.

"You always look well when you're expecting," Jessie who moved to Balmore with her would say. But her good, fresh look belied the way she felt inside. "You should see it from where I am, Jessie," she'd think to herself as she laughed too loud or made too many slighting remarks about herself.

And she always did look good. She knew that. Her hair was rich and golden, her skin was fresh and clean, her clothes were not like the clothes the village women wore. But it was more than any of these things. The real difference, the big difference lay in what was inside her. Sometimes she couldn't explain this difference, even to herself, sometimes she became confused thinking about it. But she knew she was in a place to which she did not belong. The people up here were friendly, she couldn't say that they weren't. She'd met up with a lot of it since she came here. And everyone was kind to her bairns, they were kind to all bairns. And John came from here, and John was a good man, she knew she'd travel far before she'd find better. She knew all of that. And yet, it wasn't enough, knowing. It didn't change anything. In some ways the knowing made it harder for her.

Cis shook these thoughts from her mind as she heard the clatter from the back door. Stupidness, she thought. That's all it was. Just because she was expecting a bairn.

"He's soaking," Grace said and slid little Dan from her hip on to the floor at his mother's feet. "I had to try and lift him and the pail and I'm all soaking. He wouldn't walk for me," Grace dropped on to the fender, put her head into her hands, and looked at her wet shoes.

"Did you put the pail of water on the shelf?" her mother asked her as she lifted little Dan on to her lap.

"Yes," she growled from her chest. "There's not hardly any in it." Her head came up as she became aware of the others coming in. "She wouldn't help with anything," her eyes were flames as they found Marjie.

"Just look at the state of this bairn," Cis took the hem of her apron across little Dan's running nose. "What were you doing with him?" She could wring little Dan out. Water dripped from his boots, his jumper cuffs were heavy with water.

"He fell," Marjie said and she walked over to the table.

"If she would help I could have got a whole pail," Grace fired towards Marjie. "Why does she never do anything?" she turned her red face to her mother.

"She can get the water tomorrow," her mother promised as she lifted little Dan's jumper over his head and laid it on the fender. "You're not to take this bairn again," and she loosened his boots. "Poor little soul," she said as she felt his reddened, cold feet.

"He wouldn't stay," Grace had sunk back into her mood.

Duncan edged up to Marjie's side and stared at what was on the table. Jeannie stood on the other side of Duncan. Cis looked at the three of them.

"What are you lot waiting for? Better weather?" she asked and rose from her chair. "Sit there," she told little Dan and she put him in her place. She walked to the table and lifted the sharp knife. Her other hand reached for the loaf. "You lot are getting your heads washed the night," she said, and she began sawing into the bread.

FIVE

Since coming back to live in Hilltown it was Cis' habit to send her children to visit their grandmother on Sundays. She'd scrub them down and polish them up and watch them walking down the path. The older ones were at the age when they were beginning to want to choose what they should do, and rebellion was often heard in the little house. As yet, however, Marjie and Jeannie had no thought of this rebelling. Their Grannie's Cream Soda and fruit cake was all that was on their mind. She always gave a large chunk of cake.

Marjie nearly leaped backwards on to Jeannie when her Uncle Earl answered her knock on her Grannie's door.

"Ay," he growled. "What's taking you over here at this time of the day?" He cleared his throat and fired his spittle over their heads. It landed on the white point of one of the palings. "Bothering people on the Sabbath," and he thrust his brutal head towards them. Jeannie hung back, behind Marjie, and said nothing. She was frightened of her Uncle Earl's loud voice. Marjie was frightened of him also. "We came to see our Granny," she shook in front of him. "Our mother sent us."

"Be danged," he got ready with his spittle again, but he thought better of it and instead of releasing it he swallowed it. "You'd best come in then seeing you're here." He muttered to himself again about people bothering him in his own house on the Sabbath. Marjie thought about going home but she stayed. Jeannie kept her head down so that she wouldn't have to see his face. "Mother," their Uncle Earl bellowed into the house. "Are you there mother?" and he didn't move out of their way. Marjie took a step nearer to him and reached the top step. He had spittle on his pullover.

They were glad to see their Granny's smiling face. "What are you keeping the bairns at the doorstep for?" she said to their uncle. She wasn't afraid of him. He looked at their Granny and went back into the house. "Come on in to the house," she said to them and Jeannie came from behind Marjie. She felt safe about her Granny. "That's you, maitals," she said as she ushered them inside. "You came to see your Granny," her old face smiled. "That was kind of you." They took their time about entering. They didn't want to come too close to their Uncle. Jeannie walked on Marjie's heels. Their Granny pointed to the chairs.

"Sit there now," she said and they sat on her red velvet chairs. "That's the way," and she went from them into her small kitchen. Marjie looked across to Jeannie and said nothing. They heard the kitchen sounds coming through the open door and wished their Granny would come back. Marjie shifted herself on the plush seat and tried not to breathe. Jeannie took a sideways look at her Uncle and her teeth sank into her bottom lip. She sat like a statue, the only clue that she was there was her sniffing. It sounded kind of shy and apologetic as she tried hard not to look any more at her Uncle Earl in his black chair.

"What's your father at the day?" his words were for

them although he growled into the fire. Marjie's head snapped away from the mantelpiece where she had been studying the clip of shiny brass bullets and a small brass buttoned boot. She saw her Uncle's moon face. It was shiny like the bullets and the boot.

"Oh nothing," he had taken her by surprise and there was nothing inside her head, not about her father at least. Her head was seized with her Uncle's presence. She felt hot inside because he spoke to her and doubly heatened because she knew she had said something stupid. She wished he would speak to Jeannie or that her Granny would come.

"It's him that's the lucky fellow with nothing to do eh?" and he turned to accuse the pair of them, his pale eyes searching for something that they didn't know about. "It's no many people that have nothing to do," and he turned from them. He began to make a racket from his throat again. When he had drawn up a mouthful he opened his mouth and aimed his green phlegm into the fire. It landed on the bars and boiled and spread itself there.

Marjie and Jeannie forgot to be frightened of him as they gazed at the changing shape that ran slowly and thickly towards their Granny's tiles. They watched as their Uncle reached for the poker and put it into the spittle. He tried to hook it from the bars. The spittle, however, had its own life form. It refused to come and as their Uncle tried to lift it, it strung itself out and ended up on the tiles despite him.

"Uh," he said, and there was disgust in his tone. He turned to Jeannie and Marjie from his bent position and they drew in upon themselves once more lest he think that they were the responsible ones.

"Be danged," he said, and jabbed the sticky poker into the middle of the fire.

"Is that you at my fire?" their Granny's voice floated above the sound of plates and things.

"No, nor at your fire, woman," and he kept on poking.

Silence settled over the room broken only by Jeannie's sniffing. Sometimes it was too loud and she'd try to stop altogether. Marjie could see her chewing her mouth and swallowing. Then she'd put her head down and give a quiet sniff and look to Marjie and then to her Uncle's back. Sometimes their Uncle said "Ay" when nobody had spoken. He said it once after one of Jeannie's loud sniffs and Jeannie's body jumped on the red velvet chair. She used her sleeve in her fright.

With her Uncle concentrating fully on the fire, Marjie felt brave. She turned her head towards her Granny's sideboard. Her Granny had a pink glass bowl on her sideboard. It was a strange sort of bowl. A horn shaped vase grew out of its centre. The edges of the bowl and the vase were trimmed with crinkled plain glass. Her Granny one time told her it was crystal. "You're looking at my crystal bowlie," she said. "Isn't it bonnie?" It was bonnie. They had nothing like it in their house. They didn't have ornaments there. They always got broken. They had a dog ornament once. It was a chalk dog that Colin had won at the shows and their mother liked it and put it on the front window. Then Duncan was looking for something on the window and his elbow caught their ornament and it fell to the floor and broke its head. It was no good after that, there was no glue in the house. Their father put it into the dresser drawer for when he got glue.

Marjie looked at the photographs in their wooden

frames on each side of the bowl and vase. The men in the frames were both sailors and Marjie recognised her father's nice face. She looked at her father's face for a long time, she didn't want to look at her Uncle Earl's face.

It was quiet in their Granny's house. And fine. Her furniture was as shiny as glass. Jeannie wouldn't look at the pictures of the angels which hung on their Granny's wall. She was frightened of their faces and their wings. Marjie was frightened too, but she wasn't as frightened as Jeannie was. Jeannie was frightened of anything. The angels were big on the wall, looking down with calm faces and long frocks. Marjie didn't think the angels had feet. They only had long frocks. She wouldn't let her mind think what the angels were like without frocks. She would be frightened if she saw what way their wings grew from their backs. She'd be likely as frightened as Jeannie even then.

They didn't have pictures of angels in their house. They had a picture of a big church though. Above the church there was a small picture inside a circle. It was a picture of a sad faced man with branches bent round his head. His head was cut with the branches and blood poured onto his face. She was frightened of the man's eyes. His eyes made her want to cry for him. She couldn't do that in their house so she wouldn't look at him sometimes. The Angels didn't have eyes like He had. The angels' eyes didn't bother Marjie. It was their wings. And lack of feet.

The man was The Lord. She knew that because her mother and her father knew Him. He lived in the big church below Him, Marjie thought. The big church was in England. "That church is near where I come from," her mother once told them. The Lord lived down in England. He couldn't like it very much. She asked her father one time why He had branches on His head. Her father said he would tell her when she was a bit bigger. He was Marjie's Lord too, and Jeannie's. He was likely even their Uncle Earl's Lord. When their mother had told them that the Man was Our Lord, Duncan had asked, "Is he Our Lord and all?" Then their father spoke quietly. "He's everybody's Lord," he said. "Never forget that."

"There now, you'll take cake from your Granny and the Cream Soda," their Granny was before them. She took a plate and a tumbler from the tray and handed it to Jeannie, then gave Marjie hers.

They weren't used to eating cake and they hadn't any little plates for things like that.

"Thank you, Granny," they both spoke loudly so that their Uncle would hear their manners. Jeannie didn't know what to do. She lifted the tumbler halfway to her mouth then looked at the cake. She lowered her tumbler hand and lifted the cake one. Neither went into her mouth.

"I don't know what to do," she spoke beneath her breath to Marjie.

"Take your lemonade first," Marjie nearly died on a cherry. Her Granny had played a bad trick on her there. She shuddered, water springing to her eyes and her ears as she swallowed the cherry. Their Granny sat in her chair at the fire, across from their Uncle. She looked at them, kindness beaming from her. Marjie was frightened to eat in case she would make a loud noise. She'd taken half of the cake in the first bite, never thinking that it might be other than fruit that was in it. She shrank from tackling the rest.

"You like cherries," her Granny said to her as she looked at Marjie's plate.

"Ay," Marjie croaked. "I love them."

"He hadn't fruit you know," her Granny said, and Marjie knew fine what she meant.

She decided to let the cake be for a while and she lifted her tumbler to her lips. She tried to sip instead of drinking every drop at once as was her usual inclination. It was no use. Reverting to type she tipped her head back and poured the Cream Soda down her throat in one swallow, making very loud slurping sounds after it was finished. She filled the room with her noise and even Jeannie looked at her. There was no expression under the fair dosan and her mouth was wide.

"Take your time, maital," her Granny said and she felt hotter than she had ever felt in her life. She gave her Granny a watery smile and lifted the cherry cake from the plate. She took a small bite so that her Granny wouldn't think that she hadn't any manners whatever. From the corner of her eye she caught Jeannie. She was in a state. She still didn't know what to do. Her cake and Cream Soda were up and down before her mouth like twin yo-yos and still not a crumb or sip had gone past her lips.

"Eat your cake first," Marjie hissed again. "That cake has cherries in it," she added with no feeling for Jeannie.

Jeannie sniffed and took a mouthful of the Cream Soda.

"Take your cake," their Granny said to Jeannie.

Jeannie looked at the cake on her lap and counted cherries. She trembled.

"He had no fruit," their Granny said. "It's cherries I put in it."

Jeannie took a small bite from her cherryless corner. As it went down she sniffed.

"That's the cold you have," their Granny said to her. "Have you not got a handkerchief?"

Jeannie looked at her Granny and said nothing.

"Will I give you one?" her Granny asked, half rising from her chair.

"It's the myxomatosis," Jeannie's words came rapid in her eagerness to explain. "It's going, it's going. The rabbits have it."

Her Uncle straightened his back and looked at her. Jeannie tried to push herself through the back of her chair in an attempt to get away from his face and his speaking.

"Ah, ha, ha," Marjie and Jeannie stared at him. They had never seen him laughing. "Myxomatosis indeed. Be danged," and he slapped his right thigh and turned to laugh into the fire. "Myxomatosis," they heard him repeating every now and again.

Marjie had finished her cake and lemonade and wondered what to do with the empty plate and tumbler. She looked at her plate and wondered about licking it if her Granny went back into her kitchen. Her Granny rose.

"I'll take them," and she put her hands out.

Marjie looked at the crumbs in her lap. The thought of standing on her Granny's mat filled her with consternation. In her mind she could see the river of crumbs flowing on to the floor where she stood. She wished she was home, or on the shore, or just out. Anywhere away from her Granny's shining, quiet house filled with ornaments and stuff with her Uncle hulking over the fire and spitting into it and Jeannie getting all jittery as she told about the myxomatosis.

"Are you done yet?" she asked Jeannie from below her breath.

"I'm nearly," Jeannie said. She'd given up on the sniffing because of her Uncle and her nose was running free. She was brave for all that. She pushed the last piece of cake halfway down her throat, cherries included. She nearly choked on its dryness and her Granny came to rub her back.

"That's you, that's you," she soothed and Jeannie looked up into her Granny's face. She didn't care about her snottery nose.

Their Uncle's look was enough to tell them that he was disgusted with them and that he never wanted them there in the first place.

"Never you mind the crumbs," their Granny was kind. "I'll get them with the brush." Marjie's face opened with relief.

She came quickly from her chair and caught Jeannie's arm and almost dragged her to the door.

"We'll have to be going now, Granny," Marjie said. Their Granny was at their back. "Thank you for the lemonade and the cake," she spoke for the pair of them. Jeannie was always quiet in houses. She squeezed against Marjie, and wouldn't look at her Granny.

"Chase home now. Away east with you," their Uncle's words rumbled behind them.

"Watch yourselves now," their Granny stood on her step. "You'll not go near the water now," she warned them as they left her.

"No," Marjie said. "Cheerio."

Her walk was stiff and upright until she heard the click of her Granny's door. She walked that way until she had passed two houses. Then all sign of being good because it was Sunday left her.

"I'm going home the shore way," she said to Jeannie, who was trying to hop home.

"You'll get it, Marjie. I'm telling Ma," Jeannie stopped her hopping and tried threats amid her sniffing.

"Ach, who cares?" Marjie was brave away from the house. She put her head down and ran in the direction of the shore.

"Wait for me," Jeannie screamed. She was noisy out of her Granny's house. "I'm coming too," she nearly tore her throat out with her shouting. She followed Marjie down Meg's vennel, going quickly past Meg's house in case she would see them and call to them from her door. Meg never knew what day it was and would want them to go to the shop for her.

"Marjie, come back," Jeannie's thin, high voice floated far behind her. She had reached the far out rocks and Jeannie was still standing on the bank. She hopped about the rocks like a mountain goat, her feet sure where they were going.

"I'm frightened," Jeannie cried. "You'll fall in, Marjie. I'm telling Da."

If Marjie heard Jeannie she paid not the slightest attention to her. She knew she was on the bank. She also knew that she wouldn't come down from it. She skipped and leapt over the rocks to her home. Her legs carried her from one uneven surface onto the other, skipped over pools, big pools and small pools, shallow ones and deep ones. She soared from dry bare rock to land on wet and slippery green grassy-like seaweed. She took off from the green slippery seaweed and landed on bladder wrack. And not once did she even come near to stumbling. She climbed into the air as she cleared the channel with its yawning mouth and there was a wildness in her. On the shore she found herself to be completely free. She felt this freedom and it bubbled in her throat.

Jeannie was still on the bank, still opposite her.

"Look Jeannie" — no holy ones would see her out there — "I'm the king of the castle," and she birled on top of limpets.

"You're just showing off, Marjie, you're just a big show-off thing," Jeannie shouted back. No holy ones would see her either. "I'm just telling," and she began to howl. The day was proving to be too much for her.

Marjie began to sing out on the rocks.

"My body lies over the ocean,

My body lies over the sea..........."

She stood on the other side of the channel and looked across her ocean, across to the blue hills on the other side. It must be over there that the body was laying. She imagined it, very white without any arms or legs or a head. That's the way a body was.

Jeannie was growing near demented on the bank so Marjie stopped thinking of bodies and came.

"You're making an awful racket," Marjie said and wiped Jeannie's nose with the sleeve of her jumper. It was wet anyway.

"I thought you would get drowned," Jeannie said as she stood and waited patiently for Marjie to be finished with her nose.

"You're awful daft, Jeannie. Who'd fall in?" Marjie's rough cuff nearly took her skin from her.

"Ow," Jeannie said and used her own sleeve.

She jumped down from the bank and walked with Marjie along the shore in the direction of their house. Both heads were bent towards their feet as they scanned the line they walked for any bonnie or interesting thing that the sea might have washed up for them. Sometimes they found razor shells or sea cradles or big buckies. If they lifted the big buckie against their ear they could hear the sea's sound. Once Jeannie found a blue marble and she kept it to herself, then she lost it.

"You'll be in for it," Jeannie said as she looked at Marjie's shoes.

"I'm not going to go home until they're dry," Marjie showed no concern.

"I'm wanting to go home, Marjie. My whole self is freezing," Jeannie did look a shade redder than was normal for her.

"Go then," Marjie said to her. "Nobody's stopping you." Her last two words were flung behind her as she darted towards what to Jeannie was some unknown thing. "Look Jeannie," she called and held her palm out. "That's sheep's money, pure real sheep's money."

In the centre of her palm a small, flat irregular shaped stone lay. Its colour was grey and it was shot through with a silvery substance which sparkled and glinted from it like the sunlight on the sea.

"Look at it shining, Jeannie," the stone was but a dull thing compared to the eyes that beheld it. "It's all shiny," she breathed.

"Can I get it?" Jeannie asked.

"No, you can find your own," Marjie said and her right hand formed a tight fist around her stone.

"I want to go home now," Jeannie whined.

"Go home, Jeannie, go home. And you'll never find your own sheep's money," she called as Jeannie walked up to the bank.

With Jeannie gone Marjie could take her time on the shore. It was how she liked it best, just herself and waves breaking on the rocks, with maybe a seagull or two for company. Because it was Sunday no other soul would be out.

The razor shell she found was more complete than the last one she took home. It was nearly whole, hardly broken at all. She drew the length of the shell across the fingers of her right hand. It was very sharp and she thought she had cut herself so she was careful with it after that. She found a black shiny button. It was almost as precious to her as the sheep's money and she had nearly missed it. It was lucky that she had lifted the large limpet shell. She wondered about taking the limpet shell, then decided to leave it lying. She could get limpet shells at any time, the shore was filled with them. There weren't many black buttons, however. And it was a good button, not broken or anything like that. Brand new she would say. The piece of green glass was also worth taking. She hadn't any of that colour. It looked like it might have

come from a broken Parozone bottle. She had lots of
pieces of plates. Blue and white, so calm and still, pink
and white, so soft and warm, just plain yellow, it re-
minded her of buttercups. But she didn't have any that
she could look through. She lifted it to her eye and
looked through it to the rocks, the sea and the dark hills.
For that moment they were uniformly green. She looked
down at her feet and they were green, not a salt water
mark was to be seen. She laughed then to herself on the
shore and took the glass from her eye. She looked back
to her shoes. The salt water mark was back and her
mother would kill her. She enjoyed this game she had
with herself and the glass and played it many times on
her journeying. Her heart nearly jumped into her mouth
as she belted towards the marble. It sank to her shoes
when she lifted it to find it was only a half marble. It
would have been a good one. It was blue and white, a
swirl of sky and clouds. She nearly kept it, but didn't
really want to begin collecting broken marbles. She'd
wait for whole ones.

When she found all that there was to be found on her
stretch of the shore Marjie was drawn back to the rocks.
The tide was going far out. She carefully put her
treasures into a little cranny between two large stones
and lay face down on the flat rock. She put both of her
hands into its pool and tickled the water and soaked her
sleeves. She lay that way for a long time. She was hoping
that the juntac would come from his cool place and she'd
see him crossing his pool. He was very quick, too quick
for her eye to follow sometimes. She made circles in the
water with her hands, hoping to drive him out. She knew
he was in there, whether he showed himself to her or
not. In one of the tiny cracks in the rock at the bottom

of the pool he'd be lying, his tiny eyes knowing fine what she was about. She was getting tired of waiting for him, her knees were beginning to hurt as they scraped the rocky surface. She looked about her for a stone. Not a small stone, nor one that was too large. One that was just the right size. If she sent a good sized stone crashing into the pool that would soon shift him. She'd get him to come out then and he'd be so frightened with the loud splashing noise that he wouldn't know where to go. He'd be dizzy making circles.

Through the water of the pool she spotted the very stone, one that was the right size for her hand. She put her hand through the water and felt for it, her fingers were curling around it when they stopped and she thought about what she was about to do. Scare the juntac on the Sunday. The poor juntie, he never asked her to come to his pool, or to be anywhere near it for that matter. It was his own pool. Before, the thought of him flying for his life as the stone came crashing in on him sent shivers of excitement through her, now she thought of him lying all dead on the bottom. She'd likely scare him to death. And what if someone found out what she had done. They'd tell. They'd tell anyone. And what about that Jeannie, for she'd surely have to tell her, she couldn't keep a thing like that to herself. Jeannie'd tell the world. She told the world everything. She'd say it to her mother and her father first, then she'd tell everyone. Her mother wouldn't be too bad, Marjie thought. She'd be that busy at the washing she would barely notice what Jeannie was going on about. Her tongue never stopped whatever. It was her father. She could see his face when he heard. "Are you telling me that you're right, Marjory?" and he'd speak her real name as he did when she disappointed him, "Trying to frighten a little fish. I don't know," and from the rocks she could hear his sigh. And that would be the end of her. Her father would think of the juntac first, then he'd wonder out loud to her what was sending her to the shore on the Sabbath. And she'd tell him that she didn't know.

She came from her lying position and sat on the rock, her knees drawn up in front of her, her hands clasping her knees. Her wet sleeves dripped down the front of her legs and made them colder. She didn't want to see the juntac's pool. She looked across the sea and saw nothing. The juntac and his pool filled her. She turned her head and stared into it.

What if that Jeannie told the Sunday School ones, and even the Sunday School teacher. The Sunday School teacher would find it hard to believe. "Oh, Marjie," she'd say with her face all long and straight. "I can't believe that of you." She'd be able to believe it of Arthur Morrison or James Mackay. They'd like to batter the poor little juntac to bits, right on his wee head. What if she did the same, by mistake. She shook at the thought. She'd only meant to frighten him from his resting place. She'd watch the ripples on the water growing bigger when the stone went in, she'd wait for him to dart past and he'd never come. When the water was still and she looked in she'd see him. All dead and not moving at the bottom. She'd be every bit as bad then as Arthur Morrison and James MacKay. Arthur Morrison threw big stones at anyone who walked past his house. He was always waiting at his gate with his arm raised. And James MacKay called names after wifies from his father's garden. Then he'd hide down behind the dyke. She didn't do that kind of thing. She tried very hard to be good, but just when she was trying her best she ended up doing bad. She didn't mean to do wickedness, for some reason things just turned that way on her.

The Sunday School teacher would be the worst. Worse even than her father. Her mother and Arthur Morrison and James MacKay wouldn't matter after a time. But she had to meet Miss Sullivan every week. "You know that was a very wrong thing you did, Marjie," she'd say and she'd take Marjie to stand beside her at the front, before anyone. Her mouth would keep talking and her hat would rattle to keep the time of her head. "Don't you know that Sunday is the Lord's day and on Sunday we must only perform works of necessity and mercy."

Marjie had no notion what the words meant. What was perform, and surely she spoke wrong there, it should be work, not works.

Necessity and mercy made no sort of sense whatsoever to her, they were bible words and left her stranded. What Marjie did know from Miss Sullivan's tone was that what she said didn't sound as if it had anything to do with killing a juntac who lived in a pool in the rocks.

Marjie was tired of her thinking. The afternoon was wearing on and the sky was beginning to darken and the pool appeared smaller. The juntac would never come and her neck was shivering. Her shoes and her socks were stuck to her feet, they couldn't be any wetter. She put her thought from her and thought only of the warmth of her home. As she stood against the rocks and the sky she thought of her place on the fender, felt the heat from the fire.

As she walked up the shore to the bank her feet became crystallized. The soft, dry sand stuck to the wet leather and came in around her ankles. Her mother would need to be blind to miss that, at the washing or not. She ploughed on, shutting that out. She knew she was for it but that would come when it came. Up on the bank she stamped first one foot, then the other as she tried to shake free as much of the sand as possible. When the sand stayed put she jumped up and down and flattened a nettle. The sand was still there and her feet felt scratchy. She tried wiping her shoes along long grass and some sand came off, but mostly it just stayed where it was. She gave up and walked up the vennel which would take her to their house.

Cis was taking washing from the line when she collared Marjie walking quietly through the door.

"Where do you think you've been," her mother gripped Marjie's arm and tumbled her clean clothes onto the settee.

"Nowhere, Ma. Honest, Ma," and Marjie was pulled round to face her mother.

"I'll give you nowhere, my girl," and her mother's right hand cracked her ear. "You've been on that shore. Look at the state of you," and her mother shook her.

"I wasn't, Ma. Honest, Ma," Marjie struggled to get free, like a fish from a hook.

"How many times do I have to tell you?" her mother's face was red and her hand was hard as it landed across the back of Marjie's leg.

"I was only seeing my Granny," Marjie's voice was loud with her defiance. She looked straight into her mother's face and lifted her arm across her face as she cowered low. She didn't want the other side of her face to feel her mother's wrath.

"Look at your feet. Wringing. And I can smell the salt of you."

Marjie was beat and she knew it.

"Well," she said and twisted away from her mother's reach. The fender seat was vacant.

"Come to me," her father said and her mother folded the clothes. John Clark was in his chair, deedling little Dan on his knee. Jeannie was squeezed into her corner beside him.

"What were you at?" he said when she was standing in front of him.

"My face is sore," she said and her hand rubbed the red patch.

"Lucky for you it's not your backside," he took little Dan's hand away from his hair. "Worrying your mother like that. Now, I'm warning you," and she looked at his long finger before her face. Marjie looked away from it at the rip on the arm of his chair. It was getting longer.

"How was your Granny?" her father asked.

"She's fine," Marjie spoke to the rip.

"What was she doing?"

"Nothing."

"Did she give you something?"

"She gave us a lump of cake with cherries in it and a tumbler of Cream Soda. The tumbler was nearly full," she was back with him.

"That was good," he said. "Did you take it all?"

"I took every drop," she said. "She made a mess," she looked at Jeannie whose feet were dry.

"Anyways, you'd best get that wet things off. You're

perished, lassie."

Little Dan was still making grabs for his hair.

"Will you leave?" he said to the bairn. "I'll not have a curl left with you."

Marjie crawled back to the fender.

"Mind," her mother said and she hung stockings over the brass rail below the mantelpiece.

"I saw Duncan away over at the harbour with Ian Ross," Marjie said as her wet knotted lace nearly took the tears to her eyes. "They were out on the harbour. At the very point," and she tightened the knot more. "I bet you he's not for it. He's never for it," her bad nature overcame her good intentions as she made a mess of things with her shoe.

"That's enough," her father said. "Don't talk to your mother that way."

Her mother gave her a long look. "Nothing but impudence," she said and Marjie ducked in case anything should come her way.

"Well," she said from her safe position.

"She wouldn't come home, she wouldn't come," Jeannie piped up from her corner. "She wouldn't come home from Granny's."

Marjie glared at the turncoat, and thought of what she was going to do to that Jeannie when she got her. She wouldn't escape the way the juntac did. She opened her mouth wide and jumped straight back into the battle. "But I...."

"Did I say that would do from you?" and it was Marjie he looked at.

"But she started it," Marjie fired at him.

"That'll do," there was no rancour in him.

Marjie looked at Jeannie. She thought she was good because she was with her father. She was going to be for it.

"Just be good the pair of you," their father said and he put his watch to little Dan's ear. "Tick — tock," he said to little Dan and little Dan opened his mouth wide and smiled to his father.

Marjie was disgusted with little Dan. He was always getting lifted. Jeannie thought that if she sat beside her father for long enough her mother would take little Dan and then she would get onto her father's lap. Marjie was disgusted with Jeannie. She'd copy what her father did. When he'd lift his spoon, Jeannie'd lift her spoon, when her father yawned, Jeannie'd twist her mouth, she'd walk the way her father walked and when her father smoked Jeannie'd put a pencil into her mouth and look at her father for his approval. And when her father said 'Ah' after a long smoke, Jeannie'd take the pencil from her mouth and say 'Ah'.

It used to be Marjie's game until Jeannie started doing it. She would still like to do these things but she wouldn't, not with Jeannie there first. Jeannie or little Dan was always on her Da. Her Da would lift her up sometimes but her mother would say, "What are you lifting that big lump for? Here, hold this bairn." Then Marjie would struggle from him and run to the shore.

"Where's Grace?" Marjie forgot to sulk as she spoke to her mother.

"How would I know?" Her mother was still short with her. "She went out. I think she said she was going along to your Granny's."

"Well, I never saw her," Marjie said.

"No, you wouldn't. You were combing that beach," her mother hung pants from the end of the rail.

Marjie knew the look that was on her. She held her peace.

"Move, will you," her mother's voice was ragged. "You're always in somebody's way."

Marjie slid to the other side of the fender.

"Move, I said," her mother's voice rose.

"Crivvens," Marjie said once she was out of the way. "You can't even sit in this house," and she threw herself down on to the settee.

"Is it not time they were in?" John Clark spoke to Cis, one eye on the clock and the other on the dark coming in at the window.

"They're not far," Cis said. "They'll come soon."

"Haven't you got that things off yet?" her father asked Marjie. She'd given up the battle of the laces. What did she care about wet feet anyway. "Come here to me," he said and he put little Dan from him. "Jump down, Jeannie sweetheart," and he moved his leg for her. "I don't know what to be saying to you lassie," he said to Marjie and he lifted her onto his lap. "What did you do here?" and he bent his head to his fingers as he unpicked the knots.

SIX

"I've told you and I won't tell you again, keep your hands away from your face," Cis said to Marjie as she folded her baby's nappies. She hadn't long to go and had taken the fresh day to wash and soften the terry squares. She pressed one to her cheek, feeling this softness, testing its dryness.

"I'm only rubbing them," Marjie was on the settee, her finger nails testing, picking and lifting the crustaceous top off the scabs which had formed a cluster around her mouth.

"Well, don't just rub them. You'll carry that mess all over your face," Cis put the nappies on the top of the dresser. "And keep your paws away from your head," she tapped the back of Marjie's searching hand. "You'll be a mass of corruption, you will."

"My head's awful itchy. I'm itching to death. I think the lice is at them," Marjie may have found it difficult to open her mouth because of the scabs at each corner but it didn't halt her tongue any.

"I'm going to do your head in a minute," her mother said, and she reached to the mantelpiece for a pencil and a brown envelope. "I want you to go to the shop for me," she said and she sat in her chair and began to write. Scabs, she thought. It was the last thing she needed. Jeannie was covered too and Duncan had one on the end of his chin. Who wouldn't have scabs here. The place was alive. The straw thatch under the felt was a breeding ground. And then there was the wet beds. That Jeannie and Marjie needed a cork put in them. Cis scratched her head at her thought and wrote onto the back of the envelope four plain loaves. She saw a rat at the dump when she was pegging the nappies onto the line. She thought it was a cat at first, it was that big. She shuddered at the vision that was still before her, its horrid long tail and all.

"Come on Dan. Come to Marjie," Marjie clapped her hands then held her opened arms towards little Dan. Little Dan was sitting in the centre of his mother and father's bed eating a piece and jam. Most of the jam had missed his mouth and was spread everywhere including his father's place. He opened his mouth wide for Marjie and it swallowed his jammy face.

"Come on then, Dan. That's a good boy. Come to Marjie," Marjie's face was a brown crust.

"No, he won't come like a good boy," his mother said as she wondered about bacon. "I don't want him covered in your scabs."

"You can kill fleas with hammers," Marjie said.

"Look, will you just be quiet and let me think. I can't hear myself for your tongue," Cis decided on the bacon. "My head's bad the day." Her head wasn't as bad as her back. That came with the second bairn, their Grace. The doctor had scoffed at her. "The pain will disappear when the baby comes, Mrs Clark. It's just the baby's weight pressing on a nerve. Nothing to worry about." Well, that bairn came and four more after her and another just waiting and the pain was still there. It had never left her. By, John wasn't far wrong. Doctors! What did they know. She looked ahead and wondered how John was for fags. She looked at the nappies. She'd leave them to air for a while on the fender. She laughed inwardly at the futility of what she was thinking. And after she'd aired them she'd put them away in the damp closet with the bairn's other things. The gas and air was in the closet. The nurse had left it last time she called. Nurse Cattanach was grand, she'd been with her for all of them. She laughed plenty and gave the bairns sweets. That Grace had told Mrs MacIntyre that they'd got a new gas cooker. She didn't know what the woman was talking about when she went to the washing-line. "How are you managing with your gas cooker, Missus?" Mrs MacIntyre asked as she pegged her towel on the rope.

"What cooker?" Cis was stupid as she took her baby's nightgowns from the line. "We've no cooker." Chance would be fine, she thought.

"Oh, I must have misunderstood," the woman said. "It was something your Grace told to me. 'Our mother has a new gas cooker in the closet' she said. 'We got it for our new baby'."

Cis didn't feel like laughing, but she laughed. Of course that was before the rat. "I've no cooker," she said to Mrs MacIntyre. "That's the gas and air I've got in there. It's in a big navy blue case."

Then Mrs MacIntyre dropped one of her Alec's stockings and wiped the tears from her eyes. Then Cis spotted the rat.

"I'll do your head now," Marjie's mother said to her and she put her messages note on top of the mantelpiece and lifted down a bottle of thick creamy liquid.

"Are you wanting me to put the nappies away for you, Ma?" Marjie tried to change her mother's thought.

"No, not yet," her mother said and she looked at her. Poor bairn, she thought, what a mess she was in. "That jumper's filthy," was what her mother said. "Turn it round the other way."

"What, inside out?"

"Or turn the back to the front."

"I'm wanting out. Everyone's out."

The scabs meant more than sore for Marjie. They also brought to her something which she would never have thought of. They meant that she couldn't go as she pleased. That was the way Marjie lived. Now it was waiting for ointment. Duncan never waited. He never waited for anything. And that Jeannie never waited. Just because she only had a small one below her nose.

"Alright then," Marjie said and she stood before her mother.

"I'll do your head first," Cis stuck the comb into the back of her own hair while she carefully parted Marjie's hair with her fingers. The stuff in the bottle seared the broken skin.

"Ow, that's sore," Marjie said and she tried to get away.

"Stand still," her mother said and tugged her hair back.

Cis continued her dividing of Marjie's mop, searching for any new sign whatever of eruptions. She rubbed the medication well in, her fingers felt hard and merciless to Marjie.

"Right, turn around," her mother said and took the comb from her hair.

"Oh, you're not going to comb it!" Marjie was nearly crying. "You'll comb my scabs off."

"Stand still, I said," her mother was hard and she did her best.

"Ow, you got one," Marjie was hopping beneath the comb. "And that stuff's running down my face. I could scratch it off to bits."

"Stand still," her mother said and Marjie's left cheek felt the sting from her mother's deft hand.

"Ow," Marjie howled. "You're nearly ripping my head right off."

"If you don't stand still I'm warning you, I'll give you something to cry for," and her mother finished with her head.

"Is that me all done?" Marjie asked and she was ready for the door.

"No, that's not you all done. Give me your face."

"Crivvens," Marjie kicked the edge of the mat in front of the fire. "I'll be in this house all day."

Cis lifted a small round box from the top of the mantelpiece. It had been white but was now the colour of coal.

"Give me your face," her mother dug a forefinger full of cream from the box.

Marjie wanted to laugh as she stood close to her mother and looked up into her face. She wasn't so brave that near. She felt the bubble rising in her throat and the tremors that went through her. If she let herself go her mother would skelp her and her face was very near to her mother's hand.

"Now, be told. Keep your paws off," her mother said and she wiped her fingers down the side of her skirt and put the lid back on to the box.

Marjie's face had never come nearer to looking like a cream cake.

"You're lovely," her mother said as she looked at it, and her hand went up to scratch what she imagined was crawling in her own head.

"Can I go now?" Marjie said.

"In a minute. You're going to the shop first," her mother said and reached for the envelope and pencil.

"Is it for marking?" Marjie was ready for rebellion again.

Her mother said nothing to her.

"Well, if it's for marking, I'm not going," Marjie said.

"Shut your mouth," her mother said. "You're going." She looked up from her writing. "Look, I'll give you a copper. You can get yourself a sweet."

Whatever Marjie was about to say was halted by knocking at their front door.

"There's someone knocking at the door," she said and she saw the look which spread across her mother's face.

"I heard," her mother said. "I wish your father would come in."

"Will I go to the shed for him?" Marjie felt concern for the way her mother's face went. Her mother didn't like knocks at the door.

"No, not yet." Cis rose from her chair and brushed some imaginary thing from the front of her jumper.

"Will I go to the shop now?" Marjie was ready to be away from the house.

"After," her mother said, and she crossed the room.

Cis had been waiting for the woman who stood on her doorstep.

"Can I come in?" the woman asked from her painted mouth.

'No, you can't' was what Cis thought as she let her pass.

"Don't look at the mess," she tried to keep her voice light. She hated the visits from this one. The Authorities never left people alone.

"I'll sit here," the woman said, and she brushed a hand across the seat of the wooden chair beside the table.

Marjie had crawled to the small wooden stool which was between the fireside wall and her mother's chair. She looked at the posh wifie with the pearls around her throat and the large black handbag on her wrist. She knew this wifie, she came to their house in Balmore. She saw the wifie looking at her face and she hung her head. Cis lifted little Dan and his piece from the bed and walked to her chair. She wished John was with her.

"And how are you keeping, Mrs Clark?" the woman's voice was pleasant.

"Not so bad," Cis said. She knew this one, her soft speech didn't fool her. She knew what they were out for.

"You got the clothes from the Red Cross," the wifie said. "I told them it was urgent."

"Yes," Cis said. If this one thought that she was going to make things easy for her she could have another think to herself. "Yes, they came," Cis said. 'Lovely they were too', she thought. What a ticket their Grace was in high heeled green sandals. Open toes for the middle of winter.

"Is Mr Clark working yet?" the woman asked as she pulled a small handkerchief from her sleeve and patted her nostrils.

Marjie's eyes were on her, noting her delicate way of wiping her nose.

"No, he's not working," Cis' tone grew sharp, making Marjie look at her face. "There's no work in it. For anyone," she added. Let her put that in her pipe. Sitting there cross-questioning people. Who did she think she was?

"I see," the woman said and reached to the floor for her bag.

Ay, you might, Cis thought, because I don't.

"The nurse said she found lice on the children's heads when she examined them at school. I believe she told one of them to tell you what to get to clear them. Did you manage to get the stuff?"

"I have it," there was triumph in Cis' voice as she groped for the mantelpiece and took the bottle down. "There," she said. "Their heads are done every day." That shook her closed face, Cis thought.

"You'll need more. You'll get it on prescription."

Cis said nothing. Some things weren't worth replying to.

The woman tried again. She smiled to little Dan. "What lovely curls," she said.

Little Dan's jammy face stared back at her, his eyes unblinking. She moved her interest from him and settled on Marjie. Marjie's scabby face smiled back. The wifie looked nice.

"What about that poor little thing there?" she spoke to Cis, and Marjie went behind her mother's back. She shifted on the stool. Her Red Cross skirt was scratchy.

"She's not a poor little thing," her mother spoke fiercely to the woman. "She's not a poor little thing," and Marjie caught some strange thing in her mother's voice.

"We've had a report, Mrs Clark," the woman had taken a letter from her handbag. She tapped the folded page.

"What about?" Cis asked, and she felt real dread. Her heart was going to strangle her.

"About the children. We're discussing it at the moment, but I felt I should warn you."

Cis felt stupid. What was she talking about. A report? What report. She knew nothing about reports. And what about the children? There was nothing the matter with her bairns. Little Dan squealed as his mother's grip tightened around him. "What report?" her words were thick, her tongue wouldn't work for her.

"Someone let us know that the children were being neglected," and she put the letter into her bag and looked straight at Cis. "As I've said, we're discussing the matter. There's the question of removal."

Cis was frightened. She gripped Marjie's wrist hard. "Run for your father," she said. "Hurry now. Get your father," and she pressed her face down on little Dan's head and rocked backwards and forwards in her chair.

"Well, I'll be going now. I'll be back when you've had the baby. When's it due by the way?" the woman rose and shook what ever she imagined she'd picked up from her skirt.

"You'll not go anywhere," John Clark stood straight in the doorway. "You'll go nowhere till I've had a word, my lady," and he walked into the room, crossed to Cis.

"They want to take my bairns," the tears were in her

eyes as her hand besought him.

He gripped her, and spoke to the woman.

"Listen to me," he said. "No-one is taking any bairns anywhere," and he bent towards her and thrust his face to hers. "If you or any one of you so much as lay a finger on one of my bairns it'll be the last thing you'll do. Now, get your arse out of this house and don't let me see you near it again," the spittle was boiling on his lips.

"Now, Mr Clark, there's no need for you to take that attitude. I was only saying..."

"I know what you were only saying. I know what your kind are always saying," and Marjie thought her father was going to hit the woman in the eye the way he waved his finger at her. "Coming into people's homes as if you have the right and putting fear into people's hearts."

"But I must tell you, Mr Clark, we've had a report..." the woman refused to give her ground.

"I don't care if everyone in the three villages sent you a report, there's no-one tampering with one hair of any of mine." His anger had turned to ice. He dropped his hand to his side. The woman looked at the eyes which were locked on hers. She opened her mouth, then closed it.

"Very well," she said. "I'll be going," and she scurried away from her chair. John Clark followed her to the door. "Good-bye," she said and trotted down the path to her car. John Clark said nothing. Some things weren't worth speaking to. He closed his front door.

"What if it's true?" Cis looked to him. "What if they take them?" Her voice was near to breaking.

"They won't do anything," he sat on the arm of the chair opposite. "Settle yourself, now. Think of the bairn." The carry-on had upset him more than he would ever say. If once he ever found out who had gone telling their tales he'd put a stop to them quick. He reached into his pocket for his cigarettes, stuck one between the bars of the fire. "Things'll be alright, you'll see," he said to Cis and put his cigarette to his lips. "Are you thinking of making some tea?" and he reached his hands to lift little Dan.

"Do you want tea?" Cis asked as she came to her feet.

"A mouthful, I could do with a mouthful," he said as Marjie came to stand by his knee and gripped it with both of her hands. He reached out to stroke her head and she moved from him. Her scabs were very sore.

S E V E N

"Yes, yes, speaking. That's right, it's the Postmaster General you're speaking to."

Dougal Innes was on the phone in the Post Office side of his shop when Marjie entered. Although the telephone was at the end of the other bar of the L-shaped building, anybody waiting to be served their messages could hear every word that he spoke, for he made no allowance for telephone wires and shouted across the distances at the top of his voice in case they had difficulties in hearing him.

"Yes, yes," he picked his teeth with a spent match and he inclined his ear closer still to the receiver. He was a tall angular man with great sweeps of white hair and a hooked nose. He felt the full power of his position when he was on the phone. It was that bit more elevated than selling stamps or handing out family allowances or dole money. Handing over money grieved him. No matter that it was not his, he had to put it into the hands of others and he grudged parting with every penny. At least the phone was his and it gave him status. If any of the village people needed to phone, the kiosk was there for them. They weren't like him. He was yolach with the phone, it was like an extension of himself. Most of them who came to the shop were frightened of the thing. "How much is it for you to phone the doctor for me?" they'd

ask, or "Can you come to get our Fulla for me? I have
his number on this bit of paper," those guileless eyes
would beseech him. And there were those who would
only use the phone during shop hours so that he would
be there for them.

Marjie drummed her three pennies on the counter
again. She was growing tired of waiting. When she could
still hear him talking she walked round the shop with
heavy steps so that he would stop and come to her. When
even that didn't work she opened the door and banged
it closed. It made no difference. He must be deaf and
blind she thought. A grown up would say that Dougal
Innes was as fly as a fox and knew everyone's business
but his own. She was reading the Cremola Custard
packets when he came through.

"It's yourself, Marjie," he said. "What can I do for you
the day?"

"My mother's wanting this and mark it," Marjie said
and pushed the crumpled piece of paper across the
counter to him.

"Yes, yes, yes," clicking sounds came from his mouth
as he held the paper at arm's length in front of him and
lifted his spectacles from his nose. "Yes, yes, yes," Marjie
heard him at the bacon slicer. He cut the first slice and
placed it onto the paper. He cut the second slice and
made a ball of it and pushed it into his mouth. He ate
whatever he was cutting. When he cut the corned beef
with his large knife, he'd cut a thick slice for himself.
Then Marjie wished he would give a piece to her.

He placed the bacon on the counter and put beside it
a packet of Brooke Bond tea. Marjie was collecting the
labels for a real Indian headdress with feathers, made of
real cardboard. Duncan was wanting one, but she got

there first. If her mother would buy three more packets she would have enough. Summer County margarine was good if you put it onto the two sides of your piece.

"Give me your bag," Dougal Innes said and he filled it with loaves. Then he put in the bacon and the Capstan and the tea and the margarine. After that he wrote something into a book.

"Can you manage that now?" he asked as he handed the bag down to her. The chocolate biscuits were on the top.

"Ay," Marjie said. "What can I get for threepence?"

"Penny caramels. I can give you three. Are you wanting penny caramels?" and his hand was on their box.

"How much are they please?"

"A penny each."

"Hm. How much is the lucky tatties?"

"Tuppence."

"Well, how much is the black sugars, please?"

"A ha'penny each. You'll get two of them for a penny."

Marjie knew that. She was good at sums. She thought for a while. "I'll take two black sugars and a lucky tattie," she said and she handed him her warm pennies. She wasn't sure which hand to reach up to him for her sweets, she needed both for the bag. He solved her problem for her by bending low and sticking them in between the Summer County and the bacon.

She hurried through the door, the bag bumping against the back of her legs. Once outside she dropped the bag at her feet and rammed the lucky tattie between her teeth, nearly breaking some as she bit down hard on the plastic charm embedded in its toffee. Carefully she chewed the charm loose and licked it clean. It was a green cat. A green cat would be a good thing to have. She gripped it tight in her left hand and started on the black sugar, sucking the taste from the slim black stick. She gripped the handle of the bag and began her trek home.

Her aim was to head straight along the street, back the way she had come. At Poor Benny's, however, she had a change of mind and decided to cut through the vennel. So concentrated was her mind on the black sugar that she nearly walked into Poor Benny before she had even seen him. Poor Benny rattled something at the front of his trousers and laughed at her. Marjie bent her head and hurried past, one shoe stepping into Poor Benny's pool with her haste. She took a long lick of her other black sugar, sucking its treacle taste from it, forcing the sweet tasting spittle between all her teeth, then letting it trickle down the back of her throat.

At the wooden gate which led into the park she looked up to the sky. Jocky, the farmer's black Clydesdale was at his post, standing like a sentinel on top of the farmhouse hill. Marjie was frightened of Jocky. She tightened her grip on the bag and wished she'd taken the front road. But there was no way of escape for her, no other vennel to cut back down. From the park her eyes covered the distance between herself and Jocky. She took one of her mother's chocolate biscuits. Her mother would never know and the chocolate taste went lovely with the treacle. As she bit her eyes never left the horse. She walked with care, hoping, wishing that Jocky might not see her. She kept close in to the houses and nearly landed in Old Wilson's bucket of ashes. If Old Wilson heard she'd come to her door and then she'd never reach her house. Between Jocky and Old Wilson, Marjie didn't know what way to be. She took another chocolate biscuit. Her mother would never know.

Jocky still stood on his hill. Enormous and black with a large swishing tail that reached to the ground, he had huge powerful feet that pounded the earth and rattled the houses as he bolted down from his lookout at the top. He nearly had Marjie one time before. As soon as she was through the gate he had spied her. As soon as she had seen him she flew, her heart bumping about like a rubber ball inside her. She had screamed as her house came near. And just when she'd thought she was dead he swung from her line and galloped past the dump and the well and had only stopped when he was at the pond. She'd never forget that time. Her heart wasn't right for days.

She was at Peg's house and Jocky was still up there. Peg was shaking her mat.

"What now then?" she said. "You were at the shop."

"Ay," Marjie said through a mouthful of chocolate wafer. She drew her sleeve across her mouth so as to erase any telltale traces. Her mother would know. In her state she forgot about her scabs until she felt the tears come on her eyes.

"I nearly got chased by Jocky and Poor Benny did his pee in his vennel," Marjie said to her mother as she dumped the bag on the table.

"Give it to me," Cis said from her chair. Her hand reached down the side of the bag for her list. She looked at its total and put it under the box of ointment on the mantelpiece. "Here," she handed the packet of Capstan to Duncan. "Take these to your father."

When she had taken everything from the bag she lifted the bag of chocolate biscuits in her hand. She felt their weight. She opened the crumpled brown paper bag and looked into it.

"There's never a half pound there," she said and her question looked from her eyes. "You've been eating them," and there was no question. "You greedy little witch. Always devouring whatever you're sent for."

"I never took any," Marjie's voice soared in her defence.

"You can say black's white but you don't fool me my girl," her mother's look told her how close she was sailing to a good hiding.

"Crivvens, I always get the blame for things," Marjie threw herself on top of someone's clothes which were scattered on the settee.

Her mother looked at her. "Maybe that's because you're always doing things," she said. "And straighten your chops. You'll have your scabs all cracked."

"You may as well admit it, you're just a greedy guts," Grace corked the tin of Brasso she was using on the fender and stood up. "You'd eat anything," her tone was lofty. "You can get to the well now," she waved a part of someone's vest in front of Marjie's face.

Marjie opened her mouth wide. Scabs wouldn't stop her here.

"I'm just back from the shop," her voice soared again. "I'm not going out there, Jocky's watching me. He's going to get me," and she crossed her legs and folded her arms across her chest.

"You're going," Grace said and took her duster to the big mirror on the dresser. The Brasso left streaks.

Marjie was getting tired of Grace. She thought that because she was the oldest of the girls she could be the boss. She never went to the shop, but was always talking with their mother. Sometimes when Marjie came into the house they'd stop what they were saying and look at one another and smile to one another. Then when Marjie asked them what were they speaking about, Grace'd say in her way, "None of your business," and her mother would say, "You're too small to hear." She wasn't small. Grace was only three years older than her. Grace was always polishing and tidying. That was alright. But when she expected Marjie to tidy and polish, Marjie'd run from the house. She'd stay out for hours, nearly starving to death in case Grace collared her with her 'do this' or 'go there'.

Grace was a very neat and clean girl. Her hair was never a mess, she never got jam onto her jumper, the scabs didn't even look at her. Marjie couldn't be Grace's way. Neither had she any fight against it. Her frustration reached to her heels and she kicked them against the bottom of the settee. She wished Jocky had got her and that she had eaten every biscuit that was in it.

E I G H T

Their father's foot on the stair woke them. It was early in the day, no light came in at the skylight.

"Mind your eyes from the bright," he said and he pressed the switch.

They came from their sleep, their heads broke from the blankets like the seals breaking the water around a boatman. They looked up at him, their surprise written on their sleep filled faces.

"Don't come down in the morning," he said and he bent to lift the big coat from the floor and put it over Grace and Jeannie and Marjie. "Stay here till I tell you. I'll tell you when to come."

"What's the time?" Duncan's face was the colour of chalk beneath his dark hair.

"Four o'clock," he said, already on his way from the room. "It's only four. Go back to your sleep now and keep warm," and the room was black once more.

They took their puzzlement beneath the blankets with them, and lay there, secure in their knowledge that their father was there and that he would see things right.

"Is anyone waken?" Duncan's voice floated about the

darkness.

"We're waken," Marjie said. "We're all waken, aren't we?"

"Get back to sleep," Grace mumbled from her pillow. And clearer, "Move. Jeannie, you're lying on my arm."

"Are you still waken, Duncan?" Marjie's voice came loud.

"Of course I'm waken. It's me that said it first," there was an abrasive note to Duncan's voice.

"Will you all get to sleep?" Grace said.

"I heard a car. Did anyone hear a car?" Duncan's tone changed to one of excitement.

"There's nothing there," Grace said.

"I heard a car. I think I heard a car," Marjie said.

"I never heard nothing," Jeannie's voice came small from behind Grace's back.

"I did," Marjie said.

"I thought you were sleeping," Duncan spoke to Jeannie.

"I'm not sleeping," Jeannie said.

"Will you get back to your sleep," Grace was losing her calm along with the battle. "If you don't get back to sleep you're for it," she threatened.

"Listen," Duncan appealed to them from across the room. "That's a car door banging. I knew I heard a car. What's happening, Grace?" and there was a tremour of fear in his voice.

"I never heard nothing," Jeannie sniffed.

"By God, I was right," Duncan sat upright in his bed and forgot to whisper when he heard his father talking to someone below. He heard their front door open, then close. "What's going on anyway?" he asked of anyone who might have the answer.

"You'd better go to the phone, John," the nurse came to him where he stood against the front wall of the house. "The baby's lying the wrong way."

The village slept as he walked along the street. The nurse had been in there for more than four hours. In God's name what was he thinking about? This was the end. He'd never put her through that again. Oh God, are you hearing me? Take the pain from her, take it from her, and he drove one fist into his other palm as he walked.

The doctor answered at the first ring and said he would be straight out. He sounded calm. John Clark wished that he felt the doctor's calm. The man must have driven like a madman. He came the six miles in the time John walked back home and talked to the nurse and looked at Cis. She reached her hand to him and told him not to be getting himself in a lather. Cis was strong. He went back outside when the doctor arrived.

Up and down the silent street he walked. For hours it seemed, the time went slow. He could hear the sea's murmur from beyond the shore street, could smell the salt from it. As he turned back in the direction of his house he saw the man. It was strange for anybody to be about at this hour, he thought, and he didn't see where he came out of. He was standing beside the cars. He bent to look through the window of the doctor's. He tried its door handle and moved on. He looked through the window of the nurse's. He put a hand to her door handle.

John Clark came quietly to his back.

"Ay, she's mine," he said and the fellow's hand dropped like a stone.

The stranger gave him a look, and walked east.

Duncan stood on the tips of his toes before the skylight. His vest beneath his jumper reached to his knees. A grey dawn was breaking.

"There's two cars down there," he reported to those in the beds. Little Dan was still asleep in his warm place.

"Have we got to stay up here forever?" Marjie asked him from Grace's feet.

"Have we got to stay for all of our life?" Jeannie sat up on the pillow at Grace's head.

"I'm getting bitten to death with the fleas," Marjie said.

"Are we going to school the day, Grace?" Duncan turned from the open skylight.

"No," Grace said.

"I said I'm getting bitten to death with the fleas," Marjie said. "One jumped off my jumper."

"Be quiet, you," Grace said. "You're never quiet."

Jeannie was near enough to taste Grace's wrath, so she held her peace.

"I know what I'm going to do," Duncan said. "I'm going to murder the buggers," and he walked to the landing. He lifted the lid of his father's toolbox and from the top tray he selected the claw hammer.

"Right," he said, back between the beds. "Now they're going to get it."

"Are you going to murder them to death?" Marjie squealed as she tried to walk over Grace and Jeannie to get from their bed.

"Right, watch out Grace and Jeannie," he said as he advanced, and he held the hammer above his head with his two hands. "You better get up," he said.

"I'm not getting up," Grace said. "Get back to your bed. Little Dan'll waken then we'll all be for it," and she lay there.

"I'm getting up, Duncan," Jeannie sniffed as she crawled over Grace.

"Right. I'm doing it," Duncan said to Grace. "If I bash you it's not my lookout."

"I'm coming then," Grace didn't come far. She crawled from the blankets and perched on top of the wooden headboard.

"If you get my feet you're for it," she said to Duncan. "You better watch what you're doing."

"Get up then," Duncan said, and he raised the hammer higher.

"No," Grace said.

"Right," Duncan said. "Move the blankets."

"Move them," Grace said to Marjie, and she tried to keep her feet clear.

"Okay." For once Marjie was willing. "Get them. There's ones, there's ones."

"Get them," Jeannie said.

"Right, watch out," Duncan said and he brought the hammer down on the sheet with all that he had in him. He nearly put the bed in two. "The buggers got away," he said as he looked at his clean hammer head and a spotless sheet. He tried again. This time he nailed one and nearly nailed Grace as well as his hammer flew in his hand.

"Watch where you're swinging that thing," Grace said and she crouched further away from the predator.

"Well, that's the finish of that one anyway," he said as they examined the small brown shiny thing splattered against the white cotton. "Let's do the coat," there was a note of exultation in his voice. "Lift it up somebody."

"Lift it up, Marjie," Grace commanded from her perch.

Marjie struggled with its weight until Duncan helped her.

"Put it there," he said, and they launched the coat on to the bed.

"Where will we start?" Marjie asked.

"They could be in the pockets," Jeannie said from the bottom of Duncan's bed. Little Dan was warm against her feet.

Duncan turned up a lapel and held his breath. "Look at all them," he said when he could speak.

"Is that fleas?" Marjie asked as she bent closer to the crease. Along it was embedded a solid row of the enemy. "Are they sleeping?"

"If they are they'll soon be waken," Duncan said.

"Fleas don't sleep," Jeannie said, as if she knew of such things. "Fleas jump."

"Don't let them touch me," Grace squirmed.

"I never saw them like that," the executioner sounded sad. "They're quite bonnie little things, just like honeysuckles."

"I don't know what a honeysuckle is," Jeannie said.

"A honeysuckle's a flea of course," Duncan was lofty in his knowledge.

"I think a honeysuckle's a bee, a bumbler," Marjie was

dubious.

"Well, whatever it is, this fleas is just like one," Duncan closed the matter. "Watch out everyone," and again he put all his might behind his hammer. He wiped out the whole colony, not one leapt to its own defence.

"Shake them on the floor, shake them on the floor," Grace looked as if she was going to vomit. "Don't let them touch me."

"Shake them," Duncan said to Marjie.

"I can't hardly lift the coat," Marjie said as she struggled again against its weight. "It's too heavy," and she flapped the lapel backwards and forwards as she tried to dislodge the pulverised fleas.

"Lift it right. Shake it right," Grace could fairly rattle out the orders. "Don't you dare touch me."

Marjie did her best. She pulled the big coat down onto the floor and kicked the offending part.

"Will that do you?" she asked Grace.

"Can't you do anything right?" Grace was not very gracious.

"I'm hearing a baby," Jeannie said.

"I'm not hearing nothing," Marjie said, and she continued to kick the coat.

"That's seagulls," Duncan was tired with his exertions and he left his father's hammer lying on the floor.

"You're hearing nothing. Get back into your beds," Grace said, and she was quick enough into hers.

"I'm not hearing nothing," Marjie said, and she sat on the edge of her bed. She had no breath left.

"Heesht," Duncan said and they were silent.

The sound of a strangled calling reached them, coming to them as if from some place far off. They strained to hear, but still they thought of seagulls.

"Heesht," Duncan said, although no-one spoke. The sound came again and continued longer.

"Well, it's like a wee baby to me," Jeannie said.

"It's like a wee baby to me," Marjie said, and they didn't know what they were hearing.

Duncan held his peace.

"It is a wee baby," Grace came back from under her blanket. There was a knowingness about Grace here which separated her from her brother and her sisters. "Ma got her baby," and there was a note of almost holy awe in her voice.

"Did the nurse take it in her car?" Marjie asked.

"Ay," Grace's voice was soft.

"In her black bag?" Duncan had come to sit beside Grace.

"Ay," Grace said.

"I know all that," Duncan said. "That's what Da told us."

"What'll it be?" Jeannie wondered.

"It's a baby, Jeannie," Marjie put her right.

"It might be a baby boy or it might be a baby lassie," Grace told them. "We'll know when Da comes up. You lot better get back into bed and be quiet for Ma. Her head'll be awful sore with that baby's crying."

"How do you feel?" John Clark asked Cis.

"I'm alright," she said.

They had the house to themselves once more. Things were tidy and the bairn was lying with his mother.

"Make a cup of tea," Cis said. "Then the bairns can come in."

"I have the kettle on," he said. "The milkman's past."

"Do you know I think he looks like your mother," he said from the foot of the bed. "There's a strong look of the Feeneys there," and his face was soft as he studied the tiny face. "He's a good man, Doctor Scott."

"I wouldn't be here but for him," Cis acknowledged.

"Nor the bairn," he said. "I've much to thank him for. I'll not forget."

"He said this one had to be the last," Cis' arm tightened around the baby.

"The last he'll be," he said, and his eyes looked deep into hers. "He's a fine bairn," he said. "Did you see the size of his hands? Like shovels they are. He'll be a big fellow if he's spared."

"He's beautiful," Cis said and pressed her cheek against the black downy head. "He's just beautiful," and her eyes were moist. "Make the tea," she said. "Then the bairns can come in."

"Colin, lad, are you waken?" his father put his head round the closet door. Colin looked at him from his pillow. "You have a new little brother," his father said. "Put on your clothes and come to see him."

Colin said nothing. He knew what the noise had been about. All through the night he had lain awake on the other side of the wall. He'd heard the strange voices, the door opening and closing, the cries of his mother. He'd put his head beneath the blankets then and stayed that way until the strangers went away and his mother was quiet. He was very frightened of the unnameable thing that was happening to her. He wanted to go in there and fight everyone, batter them to anything and make his mother better. Whenever she cried, he cried.

He didn't want to go through, didn't want to see what he would see.

He reached a leg towards the bottom of his bed. The cold bit at his foot and he pulled it back to its warm place. The sound that took his head from under the blankets had been like the bleat of a newborn lamb. There was a lot of that noise, then it stopped and he hadn't heard it since. His mind was afraid to ask why. He curled up tighter into himself then and tried to keep the noise from him. His father came through on the way to the back place for the pail of water one time. He pretended to be asleep then. He didn't want to see his father. He wondered about the others. Were they down yet? What way were they?

He came from his bed like an old man and pulled his trousers from the chair, laced on his boots.

Relief washed over him when he saw his mother. She looked just the same as she always did. She smiled at him as soon as he came through the door, as if she had been waiting for him. He smiled back, but couldn't speak. He wasn't used to seeing her in her bed. His mother was always working for them.

"Come on, Colin," she said and she put her hand out to him.

Colin stood awhile.

"Give me your hand," she said, and she drew him to her and he felt safe again. He looked at what was making all the noise in the early morning. It had a tiny screwed up red face, no bigger than a ball and had black hair like Grace. That's all there was to it. The rest, what he could see above the blankets, was shawl. He didn't see any hands.

"Well, Col my boy, what are you saying to this fellow?" his father clapped his hand to Colin's shoulder.

Colin didn't know what to say. "Is it living?" burst from his lips.

His mother squeezed his hand. "John," she called to him back at the fireplace. "Did you hear what this one just said?"

John Clark straightened his back. "What's that then?" he asked.

"Tell your father what you just said," his mother was teasing him.

Colin looked at the wall. He felt stupid. "I only said was it living?" he dragged the words from his mouth.

"Ho, ho," John Clark had to put the teapot down on the table. "You'll know living when this little fellow starts," he said and shook his head. "Then there'll be bagpipes in it alright."

"Has it got a name?" Colin was beginning to feel curious.

"His name's Paul," his mother said and took her hand from Colin's and touched the baby's face. "I've called him after your Uncle Paul in England. What do you think of him?"

Colin didn't know what he thought of him. There wasn't much to think of, either one way or the other. He expected it would be crying and smelly all the time, like little Dan.

"He's all right, but he's awful little," he said to his mother after a while. "Will you be getting up soon to make our dinner?"

"He'll soon grow," his mother said. "I think I'll get up in a while. I can't lie here all day," and Colin felt right again.

"He's going to be a big fellow if all's well," his father spoke to him. "You should see the hands that's on him." He put his hand on the top of Colin's head. "Anyway, I have your tea ready."

They were grouped at the top of the stair when he went into the lobby to call them to come down.

"We're wanting our tea," Marjie said.

"You can come now," their father said. "And mind your step."

Duncan led the way, his vest flapping about like a sail from the outside of his trousers. Grace followed him and Marjie and Jeannie pushed for third place.

"Little Dan's sleeping," Duncan said as he passed his father.

"We're hungry," Marjie said to him.

Jeannie smiled up at him and walked on. Grace came like one with a secret held inside her.

"What do you think of this then?" their mother said as they came around her. Grace sat on the edge of the bed and her mother put her new brother into her arms.

"Have you got him now?" her mother asked. "Put your arm around him there," she showed her how. "That's right. Support his head and his back."

Grace held him.

"He's awful little, Ma," she spoke quietly. "He's not hardly any weight."

"He'll grow, pet."

"His face feels awful soft," Grace said as she touched the velvet cheek with the tip of her forefinger.

"All babies are soft."

"He's awful lovely, Ma. Has he got his name yet?"

"I've called him Paul. After your Uncle Paul. You know, what I was telling you about," and she lifted the baby out of Grace's arms. "You'll have plenty shots of him," she said. "You lot can hold him later. He's sleeping. This little lad's had a hard time coming here for you."

"Can he speak?" Jeannie had pushed up against Grace.

"Babies can't speak, Jeannie," Marjie knew of such things. "Babies haven't any teeth," and she folded her arms across her chest.

It was what was under the shawl that concerned Marjie. All that she could see was a wee face, and it had black hair on its head. The baby made her think of the angels in her Granny's pictures. She didn't know why her mother had to go to her bed to get the baby. The nurse could easily have given it to her in the chair. Then she could keep it warm at the fire. The house was strange with her mother in her bed. And little Dan wouldn't be the baby any more. It would be this new baby. She'd never get near her father's knee now. Jeannie'd be lucky if she got on. Likely she wouldn't even get to touch the baby or lift it because of the scabs.

Duncan couldn't be bothered with the baby. It was only a baby, he had seen one before. He had seen little Dan when he was new. Now he cried to follow wherever Duncan went. He wouldn't take him, no matter what his mother told him. Little Dan's legs were too short and he couldn't walk fast enough.

"Come for your teas," their father had it poured for them. "Then you can go and play for a while. Your mother's tired."

Marjie was glad to leave the side of the bed. She'd never get near the baby anyway. Grace would make sure of that. She'd take him for herself. She licked the margarine from around her mouth. Colin sat in his mother's chair and Duncan was on the settee. Jeannie was in her place on the fender.

"You have butter on your scabs," Duncan said to Marjie beside him.

"I don't care," she said and munched the thick bread.

"I want Marjie to go to the shop," her mother put her cup on to the chair beside her bed. "Someone find me a pencil and a piece of paper."

"I'm wanting to play," Marjie said. "One of them can go," and she meant Colin and Duncan.

"Be quiet scabby," Colin said. "Do what you're told."

"Shut up," Marjie was ready to start.

"Not today, please," their father stood and looked at the pair of them. "Now, just for once let there be a little peace for your mother," and he put a hand on the table and struggled for his breath.

"Well, he called me scabby," Marjie's voice tailed away.

"Did I say that would do," he said to her. "You'll go to the shop and we'll have none of your arguing about it."

Peg was coming out of her shed when Marjie and the bag trailed down the path. Marjie kept her head down and hoped that Peg wouldn't see her.

"What's this I'm hearing?" Peg put her bucket down and leaned on the palings. "You got a new baby," her moon face beamed over the fence.

Marjie looked at her shoe kicking at the gravel on the path. She knew it. This was all she was going to hear from now on. Babies!

"I was speaking to your Dad at the milkman," Peg spoke to the top of Marjie's head. Marjie's willpower was tremendous as she kept her head down and held her tongue.

"And what do you think of your new brother?" Peg continued.

Marjie didn't know that he was a new brother, he was only a baby.

"It's fine, very fine," she rushed the words from her mouth and hurried away from Peg.

"How are you feeling now?" John Clark asked Cis. Grace had gone up the stair to straighten the beds and had taken little Dan with her. The rest were out.

"I'm not so bad," Cis said and she moved her baby to her other breast. "I think I'll be getting up when he's taken this."

"Take your rest lass when you're getting it. I can see to what's needed." He sat on the chair beside her.

"No, I'll get up for a while. The bed's uncomfortable after a while."

"Well, you know yourself. But there'll be plenty of time for up."

They looked at him, at the small mouth seeking for life.

"The last one," John Clark said. "And to think that we nearly lost him." And yourself too, he thought, but he let that pass. He looked at his son at the beginning of his life, and he saw his life, and in his heart he asked the Lord to keep him. The little eeshan put up some fight though, nothing was going to stop him. And now here he was as nice as you please sucking away at his mother as bonnie as could be. And Cis was only talking of rising.

"We've seven bairns," she said to him. "Seven's just fine."

"Seven's more than fine," he said. "Seven's plenty I would say," and he tried to make a joke for her. Ay, he called the doctor many's a thing in his time. He'd be the first to admit that. But what that man did for them this day he would never forget.

N I N E

June was boiling, turning the tar on the road to treacle, peeling the tender skin from young necks and noses, spreading her freckles over pale faces. The rose bush which grew near to the school was bursting with its small pink blooms, the heavy cloying scent of the yellow blossoms on the whins was all around them and over them and filled them. The sky was high and blue and far away.

"What does yours say?" Kathleen, now living in her Granny's house in Hilltown asked Marjie as they walked from school that day.

Marjie read from the sheet of paper which she held in her hand. "It says I've passed my qualifying exam and I've to go to the Academy for five or six years. And I'm going to be taking French and Latin."

"You're the only one from Hilltown that's going to the Academy," Kathleen said.

"I know. Two from Balmore's going. James MacLeod and Anna Vass."

"And what did you get your books for?" Kathleen was still starched and freshly ironed looking at eleven.

Marjie slid the black book with the gold edged leaves from its slip cover. "This is my bible," she said and she opened it at the first page. 'Presented to Marjory Elizabeth Clark' she read aloud. 'First Prize for Bible Knowledge.'

"And what's the other ones for?" Kathleen asked.

"For being first," Marjie said. "This one," she showed the book, with the wild looking dog with big teeth that would rip you on the cover, to Kathleen. "Silver Chief, Dog of the North by Jack London," she read from the cover. "And this one," she said, "is King Solomon's Mines by H. Rider Haggard. You get two books when you're the Dux."

"Are you the dux of the school, Marjie?" Kathleen asked as they walked.

"The girl dux," Marjie answered, her books held close against her chest. "James MacLeod's the boy dux."

"What will I do when you leave, Marjie?" Kathleen wanted to know. "Who'll help me then?"

Marjie looked at Kathleen and wondered how her mother got her dresses to stay out the way they did. "I can still help you," she said. "I'll come to your house."

"Will you?" Kathleen's eyes were grave.

"No bother," Marjie promised, and they walked in silence until they came to the top of the brae.

"Do you think you'll like the Academy, Marjie?" Kathleen asked.

"Surely," Marjie told her. "You get lots of stuff there. They teach you maths and science," Marjie said, her voice quickening with her excitement. She hadn't a notion what maths and science were and tended to speak them as one word, but she was more than willing to find out.

"I would be frightened," Kathleen said. "They fire ink pellets at you and push your head down the toilet."

Marjie's mouth dropped open at the picture the last gave her.

"Huh," she said to Kathleen. "Just let anyone try."

"Will you miss our school?" Kathleen asked.

"Ay," Marjie said. And she would. For it was true what Kathleen had said. Our school. It was Kathleen's school, and it was Marjie's school and it was the school of every bairn that came out of the villages. Their school, built for them. Theirs of right. They were never incomers, they had their places from the start. If Marjie would stop long enough she would acknowledge that the Academy was a daunting prospect, as well as exciting. But whenever that side of it surfaced in her mind she pushed it from her. She wouldn't think that way.

The Academy was the high school of a wide area. As well as taking the secondary pupils from the town in which it was situated, it caught the eleven-plus passes from the surrounding villages and farming districts. Pupils had to travel six miles on the bus from Balmore and Hilltown. Only the town dwellers walked there, and to them, of course, it was their school.

"You better not take anyone's seat on the bus," Kathleen advised.

"All the big ones have their seats booked. No-one's allowed to sit up the back." Kathleen seemed to know a lot for someone who was never going to be going to the Academy.

"Well, I'll just find my own seat," Marjie knew the way

her friend was. None of Kathleen's talk put her up nor down. "And if anyone touches me they're for it anyway," and Kathleen knew what that meant.

"Ay, Marjie, you passed your qualifying," Ian Ross told her as he raced like a hare towards the brae, bare brown legs flashing in the sun. He'd be in the sea before they even reached the brae's foot, and all without stopping for a breath.

The secondary girls walked slowly with heads together and whispered of things, amid sidelong glances at the secondary boys. The secondary boys didn't know the girls were in it and they punched each other on the way home.

"What book did you get?" Duncan, belting to catch Ian Ross, pulled himself up.

"That and that and that's my bible," Marjie showed them to him.

"What one did you get?" Marjie looked at the book rammed into his jacket pocket.

"Twenty Thousand Leagues Under the Sea," and he clapped it hard. Kathleen still didn't know what way to be about him. She stood behind Marjie and looked at the road. The sun had worked well on Duncan's face, and it looked like one solid freckle. The haircut which Alec MacIntyre had given to him for the prizegiving was a divot on top of his head. What did any of it matter to Duncan? School was finished for six whole weeks, the sun was blazing, and the sea was waiting for him. And he had taken a prize.

"Right," he said, because he didn't know what to say, and he sped off. He pulled up again after he'd run a few yards. "Are you showing Granny?" he called to Marjie.

"If she's at the door," Marjie shouted out to him. "I'm not going in."

Grace and another big girl passed them. Grace looked at Marjie, but she said nothing. Marjie watched her dark head nodding up and down to her friend's sandy one as they walked.

Her mother was singing her song as Marjie walked up the path. From the open door and window the words floated over the lupins to her.

'We'll gather lilacs in the spring again

And walk together down an English lane'

The day was proving good for her. First the prizes and the summer day, now her mother singing.

"I want you to go to the well for me," her mother was twisting clothes over the tin bath. "I've loads to do yet and no water."

"I got my prizes," Marjie said.

Her mother pulled a towel from the mantelrail and wiped her hands.

"Show me," she said and lifted her heavy hair from the back of her neck.

"Is there anything in it? I'm starving," Marjie said and she gave her mother her two books.

"When I'm finished," her mother said, reading what was written on the fly leaf of one.

"Crivvens," Marjie groaned. "You'll be ages yet."

"Yes, I'll be ages yet," her mother was on the next book.

The promise of the day was fading for her. "Well, can I get my books then?" her tone was ungracious.

"Show me that," her mother said, and reached forward her hand for the sheet of paper.

"That's about me going to the Academy," Marjie said.

"Well, give it to me. I want to see what it says." Her mother's hands looked swollen and wrinkled from too many washings.

"Duncan's second in his class," her mother handed the paper back to her then began to thump whatever it was she had in the water. "Put these away and then you can go to the well."

"Where's Da?" Marjie asked.

"Where he always is, in the shed," her mother said without looking up from her work.

"He's not in the shed. I looked."

"Then how should I know where he is?"

"I was wanting to show him what I got."

"You can show him later. You can get yourself for my water."

"Where's everyone then?"

"Out." Her mother stopped what she was at and looked at the face looking back at her, read the mutiny spread across it. "Everyone's out," she said and there was the weariness of the world in her voice. "Everyone's cleared off. So you can get yourself to that well my girl."

Marjie looked at her mother and read what was there. She bit back what she had been about to say.

"Well, nobody better touch my books," she said as she put them on the top of the dresser. She'd never forget her last year's book. *Little Women*. She couldn't wait to find the peace to read it. It had lasted two days. Then little Paul got his hands onto it. When she came back from the shore there wasn't much more than the cover

left. Her mother had given her the row and told her it
served her right for leaving things lying about. If anyone
touched this books they'd be for it, she thought as she
lifted the pails from the shelf.

"That's you done of the school for the summer, Marjie
maital," Mrs MacIntyre was coming from the dump with
her basin in her hand. She walked slowly, awkwardly in
the heat.

"Ay," Marjie said and she set the pails down on the
grass. As she got older she was able to carry more and
the water came about three-quarters of the way to the
brim.

"Ah well, you're a good help to your mother." Mrs
MacIntyre took her hand from her apron pocket and
tucked a stray strand of her hair behind her ear.

"I'm going to the Academy after the holidays Mrs
MacIntyre," Marjie said. "I passed my qualifying exam."

"Ow vow, are you telling me that," the old woman's
eyes creased with her joy. "It's a scholar you'll be."

"You get French and Latin there," Marjie said. She
kept quiet on the maths and science. She didn't think
Mrs MacIntyre would know what they were. "You can
get German when you're in third year." Already she felt
different, using strange words like 'third year'. That was
the way you said it when you went to the Academy. In
Hilltown school you said class three, like the little ones.

"Well, bless me Marjie. To think you'll be speaking all
that foreign words," and she bent low to Marjie and

clapped her hand to her shoulder. "Your mother and father must be very proud of you."

Marjie was shy at such praise. She wasn't used to it. She lifted her pails and walked with Mrs MacIntyre to their back doors. At hers, Mrs MacIntyre paused. "Just wait till I tell Alec," she said.

"There's not enough there. You'll have to go for more," her mother's front was soaked with wringing the clothes.

"I'm wanting to go out to play," Marjie said. "Kathleen said she would call for me."

"Never mind Kathleen," her mother said and she tipped the water into the big black pan and filled the kettle.

"You've plenty water there," Marjie said.

"I haven't got plenty water," her mother said. "I've all these to do yet," and she nodded to the heap on the floor at her feet.

"You're always needing water," Marjie felt she was safe because her mother's hands were buried in soapy water.

"You little witch, don't you stand there and cheek me," her mother said and the bar of carbolic flew through the air and cracked her on the right temple.

"Ow," she squealed. "That's sore."

"If you don't get out of my sight and to that well I'll give you something that'll be really sore," her mother threatened.

Cis' back was killing her. One day she would collapse into this bath, she thought. And not one of them would notice. 'I'm starving. Is there anything in it?' they'd crowd around her to ask.

"This is all I'm going for," Marjie said. "This is all I'm ever going for. Someone else can go in future," and she tried to tear the handles from the pails when she gripped them. There was no arguing with a cake of carbolic.

"And you can get me my soap," her mother said as she was ready to glide through the door.

"I need wood for this fire. It's nearly out," her mother said when she put the two other pailfuls in front of her.

"Have you not got any?"

"I haven't any."

"None at all?"

"None at all."

"Crivvens."

"Never mind crivvens."

"Is Da back then?"

"He's in the shed. Him and Jeannie."

"Can I show him what I got first then?"

"Go, then," her mother screamed. She gripped the side of the bath. She was going to fall. "But I want those sticks. None of your clearing off. I know you."

"Ay, and I know you," Marjie muttered beneath her breath as she lifted her books off the top of the dresser.

"I heard that," her mother said, the water dripping from her forearms.

"I never said anything," Marjie said and walked out the door.

Jeannie was sitting on the stool Colin had made in his last year in school. Their father was on his old chair. He looked up from the line he was cleaning.

"That's you," he said to her at the door. "We were waiting. Was your mother needing you?"

"I had to go to the well," Marjie said. "She's doing the washing."

"So you went for the water?"

"Ay, twice."

"That's good," he said, and he pushed a hook through its cheepich. "I was just going to finish this bit. But if you got enough."

"I got plenty," Marjie said, and she waited for him to say about her prizes.

"I wasn't here when you came," he said.

"I know."

"I took two or three lug to Alec. He's going to try his scountrach," and he wiped his hands on the knees of his trousers.

"Show them to me then," he said and reached his hand out.

"Well," her voice was quick, her eyes had that light. "This is my bible. I got it for first in Bible," she explained for him.

He tipped the book from its cover onto his other hand. He felt it with his fingers, turned it over then back again. Then he opened it. Marjie was impatient with him. She wished he would hurry, she wished he would speak. He read the words they had written out loud, taking his own time with each word. She watched his mouth making the words. And when he'd finished she felt a warmth around her that had little to do with the day that was in it.

"My word, but that's lovely," he said and he handed it back to her.

"It's big eh?" Marjie's voice held a note of eagerness.

"It's a good size, I'll grant you that. See and make use of it now."

She put her hand out for the bible and handed over the two books. Again he read what was written inside, taking the meaning of it into himself. "Dux of the school, eh? You're a very clever girl. Now, I'm telling you."

She looked away at his praise, she didn't know what to do with it.

"And what have you got there?" he nodded to the sheet of paper.

"It's to say I go to the Academy," she said and handed it to him. Again he read aloud and Jeannie, her head to the side, listened.

"You keep those safe now," he said. "Put them by somewhere." He too was remembering the how-do-you-do with the prize books last summer. "Dux of the school, Marjie girl, and speaking French and Latin words eh? What are you saying to it?"

"I don't know," Marjie said, and she looked at him.

"Anyways, you be a good girl and go for one or two sticks for your mother. We'll get the coalman in the morning."

"I better go then."

"That's it," he said. "And mind what I said about putting your books in a safe place. Give me some more line," he spoke to Jeannie.

Jeannie fed him the line from the basket and his swift

sure hands worked on.

Marjie felt the goodness come back into her day. Her
father thought her books were fine. Her hand went out
to stroke the lupins as she walked up to the house. This
time she didn't pull their heads from them. The good
day started with the teacher. She told the class about
Marjie. And at the prize-giving the headmaster talked
about her marks. Her head was like a balloon. Then
there was Mrs MacIntyre. She wouldn't count Kathleen,
she was worried about her homework. And her mother.
Her mother would never say much, but Marjie knew the
way her mother felt. And now her father.

"Are you coming the day or tomorrow?" her mother's
voice came through the window to her. "I can't wait all
day, you know."

"I'm coming," Marjie said and she took the top from
a pink lupin.

For a while some things had changed. But only for a
while. She still had to go to the well, and to the shore
and likely even it would be her that was sent with the
slop pails. Fancy French or Latin wasn't going to alter
that.

"You took your time," her mother said, a pile of twisted
clothes heaped in the basin in her hands.

"Where's the bag?" Marjie asked. The sparkle had left
her.

"Where it always is," her mother said and she walked
through the closet door to the washing-line.

Marjie opened the door of the dresser and pulled the jumpers and tumblers to the front. She put her books and the sheet of paper far to the back of the top shelf and covered them with the jumpers, and put the tumblers on the top. Then she went ben to look for the bag.

Her father had many bags and she didn't know which one she should take. She lifted one up and looked at it. It had black writing in the centre of it and a black circle. It was the bag Duncan won the sack race with. It came from the farm.

"Marjie. Marjie," she took her head from the cupboard and listened. The calling came again. "Marjie. Are you coming out Marjie?"

Marjie went to answer the call, the potato sack still with her.

"Are you coming out?" Kathleen stood there in her good school clothes and red sandals.

"No," Marjie said. "I've to get sticks. I'll be for it if I don't."

"Oh, come on Marjie. Tell your mother you'll go for the sticks after."

Marjie looked at Kathleen. If she were to tell her mother anything she knew what she would get.

"She's needing them now," she said. "I'll have to go."

Then Kathleen tried another ploy. "I got sixpence from dad," she said. "I'll buy you an ice lolly."

Marjie was beat. "Alright then," she said. "Wait till I put this bag back."

"Haven't you gone yet," her mother collared her just as she was shutting the cupboard door.

"I'm just going out with Kathleen for a while," Marjie said, and waited.

"You're not going out anywhere with anyone," her mother was at her back with the empty basin.

"Kathleen'll hear all that shouting," Marjie said. "She's just at the door," and it was herself who was making the most noise.

"Let her hear," her mother's voice had risen also. "I don't care if the Queen's at the door."

"What a house this is," Marjie floated through the door, the bag following her like a parachute. "Always bawling," she called back to her mother from the safety of the doorstep.

"Get out," her mother screamed, loud enough for the street to hear, and Marjie was remembering the cake of soap.

Whatever came out of Marjie's front door put nothing on Kathleen. She was long used to Marjie and the ongoings of her family. Ever since their days in Balmore. Back there Marjie's mother didn't shout the way she did now. In the beginning it startled Kathleen and one day she asked Marjie, "How is your mother always shouting?"

"I don't know," Marjie had said then, and clamped her lips.

Marjie decided to do her gathering at the other end of the village. That way she could walk Kathleen home and get the ice lolly. Then she could cut down to the harbour.

"Your mother shouts," Kathleen said it again as they walked through the village.

Marjie said nothing. Her mother's shouting bothered her a lot more than she would say, more than it bothered Kathleen. Kathleen's mother didn't shout. Hers was a quiet house. Kathleen tried again. She took the sixpence from her frock pocket.

"Dad gave me this," she showed the sixpence to Marjie.

"You told me," Marjie said.

"Come on," she said when they reached the shop.

"I don't want to," Marjie said, and she looked to the distance.

"Come on, Marjie. Leave your bag," Kathleen giggled.

That was another thing about Kathleen. Her mother and her father were always Mam and Dad to her. No matter who she was speaking to. It was always 'Mam said I could do this', or 'Dad and me were at the lobsters'. She spoke easy, in a natural way. Marjie never called her mother or father Mam or Dad. In her thought they were her Ma and Da. And that's what they were when speaking to her brothers and her sisters. When relating something to her Da it was, 'Ma said', and when telling her mother something it was 'Da's wanting'. To her friends, however, and to anybody outside the immediate family it was 'My mother' and 'My father'. She noticed this difference most markedly between herself and Kathleen, but it was there with others also. And it was the same with the rest of them. She didn't know why it should be like this, the short pet names just didn't come easy.

"Are you coming then?" Kathleen had her hand on the nob of Dougal Innes' door.

"Alright," Marjie said and left her bag on the pavement.

The shop was empty and Dougal Innes was leaning on the counter, adding up sums in his big brown book.

"Can we get two ice lollies?" Kathleen spoke to him when he made no sign of looking up.

He sighed and drew a line with his pencil under his sum.

"You're lucky," he said from the depths of the freezer. "I've only three left. We're sold out."

Marjie looked at his bent headless form. "What kind have you?"

"There's two orange and one red one," he said.

"Have you not got any green ones?" Marjie's sigh was audible to him through the icy walls of the cabinet.

"I told you," he said. "Only orange or one red. Make up your mind. It's freezing in here."

"I'll take red," Kathleen said. "You'll have to take orange," she said to Marjie.

"I was wanting green," Marjie said.

He came up from the depths with two ice lollipops in his hand. "You'll have to take them," he said and he held out the orange and the red. Kathleen put her sixpence into his outstretched palm and took the red. "You'll have to take the orange," he got in before Marjie had time to open her mouth. "We're sold out with this heat," and he took his hand over his face.

"When will you be getting more in?" Marjie asked as she took the orange lollipop.

"He'll not be here before Thursday," he put the sixpence into his drawer. "I'll get nothing till then. I have only one block of ice cream left."

"Will you be getting green ones in on Thursday?" Marjie asked from a frozen mouth.

"Likely," he said. "I only have one block of ice cream left."

She thought then that he was going to start crying. She wished that she had never spoken about the ice lollies.

"I'm going to need a hand in the shop for the holidays," he said when they were going through the door. Marjie looked at Kathleen, enquiry in her eyes, wondering why he should be telling this to them.

"Do you think you could help me out Marjie?" he said.

Marjie turned to face him. She crunched the orange ice and swallowed it.

"You mean serving?" she asked.

"Yes. Now that it's the holidays I'll be kept busy with the holidaymakers and their bacon and people coming in for their rolls," and he picked something from between his teeth.

"When would I come?" Marjie asked from orange lips, while Kathleen giggled at her back.

"Start Monday," he said, examining what he found in his mouth. "Be over for when the shop opens."

"Would I be there for the whole day?" calculations were going on inside her.

"Yes," he sounded surprised at her question. "Yes, yes, yes," he said. "I'll give you two pounds and ten shillings for the week to Saturday. Half a day on Wednesday mind."

It wasn't to be denied. Two pounds and ten shillings was a lot of money. It would be a good help to her mother. And there was a school uniform to be got from

somewhere. Of course she wouldn't see the holidays but
there was the half a day on Wednesday and there was
Sunday. Sunday wasn't much good. Nobody came out
on Sunday.

"Ay, yes, alright," she said. "I'll come on Monday,"
and she pushed Kathleen through the door before her.

Marjie wanted rid of Kathleen so that she could think.
Her kindness in buying the ice lolly was a thing of the
past, pushed from Marjie's mind by the news she was
carrying.

"Do you know how to serve?" Kathleen still had half
of her lollipop left.

"Of course," Marjie was brave. "Anybody knows how
to do that."

As they walked along Marjie wished that Kathleen
would eat her lolly and stop her birling about and leave
her in peace. For there was plenty to think about. Two
pounds and ten shillings would get her anything. Maybe
she wouldn't have to give everything to her mother. It
was the slicing machine that worried her. What if she
took her hand off? Or even a finger. What if her finger
fell on top of some wifey's bacon when she was cutting
it for her.

"What about how much things are?" Kathleen asked,
taking a long lick.

"Dougal'll tell me," Marjie's lolly was finished before
she left the pavement outside the shop. She wasn't going
to let Kathleen put a damper on things for her. She just
better not say about the slicing machine.

As they drew near to Kathleen's house Marjie was thankful yet again that the bubbly jock was dead. When she and Kathleen lived in Balmore they would sometimes cut down the brae to visit Kathleen's Hilltown granny. She was a kind little wifie who always gave them good things to eat. That's if ever they managed to get past her bubbly jock. It paraded along the front of her house and flew at the legs of anyone approaching with huge white wings spread and a horrible squawk coming from its throat. It caught Marjie's ankle too often. While Marjie was screaming and running in circles Kathleen would dodge into her granny's. Then the granny would appear from her house with her big stick and beat about the bubbly's head and chase it from Marjie. She'd take Marjie into her house and tell her to sit on Kathleen's special little chair. Kathleen was kind and never said a word about Marjie getting her chair. She'd sit on one of her granny's other chairs and smile to Marjie. When Marjie was living in Hilltown and Kathleen and her mother and father were still in Balmore the old granny died and the bubbly jock got killed too. Now Kathleen lived in the granny's house with the little chair and it was quiet.

"I can play on Wednesday," Marjie said to Kathleen as they took their parting. "I can come out on the half day."

She threw the bag onto the harbour and made for the rocks. The tide was far out so she headed for the flat rock with the deep well. There she lay on her front and looked into the mirrored surface of its pool, feeling the

pleasurable warmth of the sun on the back of her legs.
She lowered her head to the pool and let the ends of her
hair trail in its water. If she put her face lower, her nose,
then her whole face, could feel its cleansing coolness. It
was the most beautiful thing she had ever felt. She wished
she could remain about the pool forever but her mother
would be waiting for the sticks. She learnt about other
pools in school, ones that were bright and deep. Her
pool was that way. And she learnt about where the grey
trout lay sleeping. She didn't know grey trout. She knew
salmon, and haddies and sooyans and sellacks. Even the
juntie. But she didn't know grey trout. One day she was
going to find that lea in the poem. It sounded a good
place to be.

She came from the pool and took her bag from the
harbour. She was halfway towards home and still she had
little to show. She should have stuck to her own stretch
of shore. There were too many people gathering the
same thing at this end she thought. It was good luck that
she found the big lump of tree. It was so heavy that she
had quite a task in manoeuvring it into the bag. Bent to
her gatherings she let her mind wander once more.

Two pounds and ten shillings. She tasted the words
and they were good. At the tatties she had made seven-
teen and sixpence a day, but she didn't count the tatties.
That was hard work and nearly broke her back. All she
would have to do for this pay would be to stand behind
the counter and cut ham and give wifies Bisto and stuff.
And she'd smile to Poor Benny. "What would you like
the day?" she'd say to him. She'd have to try to keep
herself tidy though. That might be hard.

She continued her gathering, finding only small pieces
that the tide had brought in. At Beulah's she sat on the

bank to catch her breath, the bag humped beside her. It was nearly filled, or at least it was nearly half filled. Maybe it would be enough for her mother. It was good that she found the big lump of tree.

It was just as she was studying the cootie on the sellack rock that she remembered The Teacher. The cootie wore his single black and looked like the old men on Sunday.

Who would do the jobs for The Teacher when Marjie was in the shop? She could ask Jeannie. Jeannie'd go for the sixpence. Or maybe even Duncan might go. Or maybe not Duncan. He scoffed when he heard what she did to earn the sixpence.

"All that for sixpence. You're off the head," but it didn't stop him begging from her what the sixpence bought.

Her mother was still at the washing when she returned. The soapy suds flowed over the side of the bath and made a pool on the linoleum.

"There's your sticks," Marjie said and hauled the bag across the floor.

"Give me them," her mother said and she tipped the sticks at her feet. She threw a handful of the small pieces on to her dying fire. Then she lifted the large piece. "That's no good," she said. "It's full of water."

Marjie looked at the chunk. She had dragged the weight of it all the way for nothing.

"I got a job," she said from the arm of one of the big chairs.

Her mother was back at the twisting and squeezing.

"I said I got a job. Are you hearing me?" Marjie said.

Her mother's hands stopped and she raised her head.

"Dougal Innes asked me. I've to start in the shop on Monday."

"How much is he paying you?"

"Two pounds ten a week. He's wanting me for the whole holidays."

"That's good," her breath was heavy. "That's good," she said.

"Are you wanting me to put that out for you?" Marjie looked at her mother bent there and the old unnameable fear pressed its finger on her.

"No, no I'll do it. It's the last, thank God. Get yourself something to eat, then go and tell your father about your job."

"Ay, O.K.," Marjie said and she walked to the table and the loaf.

Jeannie was still on Colin's stool. She'd stay in the shed and never see the holidays as long as her father was there and he had work for her to do. Her father had finished cleaning his line and had begun on the baiting. He was taking a break, his cigarette was in his hand. There was no break from Jeannie's tongue, however. When she got started she forgot to stop at all and she rattled on like an express train. This time it was about wanting plaits in her hair. Her friend had one hanging down her back. What did her father know of plaits and things? What he did know was that you required hair for that sort of things and Jeannie didn't have enough.

Marjie waited till she stopped talking about the plaits then jumped in before she could start on anything else.

"I just came to tell you," she said to the two of them. "I got a job working in Dougal's shop. I'm starting there on Monday."

"When did he speak to you?" her father said, not sounding the least bit surprised.

"When I was going for the sticks over Kathleen's way. We were in the shop."

"And how much did he say that he would pay you?" he flicked ash from the end of his cigarette.

"Two pounds ten shillings a week," she said.

"He thought for a while and seemed to do his sums in his head. "Well, I think that would be alright. What does yourself say?"

"I would like to work in the shop. And I'll give all my money to Ma," she shook her head to frighten away the bee that was looking for her. "I only have to go for a half day on Wednesday. I could play then and at night."

"It'll be a help to your mother in any case," he said and, his cigarette smoked, he picked up a lugworm from the enamel plate on his lap and pushed it into a hook. "It'll be a big help," he said.

"Jeannie," Marjie spoke to her over her father's head. "Will you do The Teacher?"

"I don't know what to do for her," Jeannie said. If her forefinger was pushed any further up her nostril her left eye would land at her feet.

"It's easy," Marjie dismissed the tasks which she found hard enough to do. Some Saturdays she'd be over there for nearly two hours.

"What will I have to do?" whatever she found up her

nose disappeared into her mouth.

"I clean her fire out first. You have to put the ashes onto a paper. You always have to put the papers down in case her mat gets dirty."

Jeannie thought on this. "Hasn't she got any pails for her ashes?"

"She has pails but they're for the coal. You only put the coal in them. You'll get heck if you put ashes in."

Their father worked steadily on, paying no heed it seemed to what was going on around him, his head bent to his work.

"You roll the ashes up in the paper and put it into her dustbin. That's at her back door," Marjie said.

Jeannie thought some more on this. She was trying to work out how to roll up a paper that had ashes in it. "How has she not got pails?" she asked.

"I don't know how she hasn't pails. Some people don't have pails, they have dustbins. With lids on," Marjie was beginning to lose her patience with Jeannie.

"Uh," their father said and he shook his hand and put his thumb into his mouth. They looked at him, then back to one another.

"Then I break the morning fire sticks for her. She has a cardboard box for them. It usually has some in it, so just fill it to the top. They have to do for the whole week."

"Where will I get the sticks," Jeannie was cleaning out her right nostril.

"She has blocks in the shed. That's where she keeps her axe too. It's lying beside the blocks. You can't miss it. And fill the two pails with coal. And take in a box of blocks for her."

"She doesn't want much, does she," their father's voice

was quiet at the baiting.

"I don't know where to take that stuff to," Jeannie said.

"Just leave them inside her back door."

"Is that all?" Jeannie asked. She was spent just listening.

"Is that not plenty?" their father said.

"She might ask you to shake her mat before you go."

"I don't know how to shake mats," Jeannie's bottom lip sagged.

Marjie rolled her eyes to the roof of the shed. "Anyone can shake mats," she said. "You just shake them. Will you go then?"

"Ay, O.K."

"You better be over there for the right time. I'm telling you, Jeannie, or you'll be for it. You go over at ten o'clock. She'll be up then."

"I know," Jeannie said and screwed her finger a little further up her nostril.

She wasn't worried about the coal or the sticks or even about using the axe. She could use an axe. She was nine. It was putting the ashes into the paper and keeping them there that was bothering her. What if she didn't roll it tight enough and the ashes landed on The Teacher's mat. She shook at the thought and her finger probing took the tears to her eyes.

"Give me more line," her father said.

As Marjie skipped along the top of their dyke she wondered if she could trust Jeannie. At ten o'clock next Saturday she would be in the shop, so someone had better make sure that she went. If no-one was in the shed she'd climb up on the palings and reach the roof. Then she remembered the last time. Her mother had caught her at it when she was talking to Peg at the front door. Her mother had given such a shout that she jumped from the shed to the palings, and with her hurry she left half of her frock looped over them. She heard that story for many days after that.

The houses over the road sat white in the sun, the dusky scent of the lupins hung heavy on the air, the sounds of children's voices came over the roofs from the park at the back. She would like to play football, she liked to run with the ball, she was fast, but she'd only end up in the goals again. Duncan always said the same thing when he saw her. "Here's Marjie coming. Great. She can go in the goals." She wasn't going to be in the goals for them today. She'd only get all of the blame for not stopping the ball. She could stop the ball if she wanted to. Any time. No bother. She didn't need any of Duncan's lip.

"Can't even save one goal," he'd follow her from the field when she walked away through boredom. "Not even one old goal," he wouldn't stop even when they were in the house. "Arthur Morrison only let two in for the other ones," and he'd push his freckled face against hers, as the words tumbled from his mouth.

"I don't care," she'd defend herself. "Who cares anyway?"

Duncan needn't come looking for her the day. He could go in goals himself if he was that bothered.

Jeannie and The Teacher came back in on her. That Jeannie better do things right. Then there was the shop and the slicing machine and keeping herself clean. There was plenty to eat in the shop.

She shifted her self on the stones of the dyke. Kathleen said they pushed your head down the toilet in The Academy and then pulled the plug. She didn't like the sound of that although she would never say to Kathleen. She wouldn't go near a toilet when she was there. That way she would be safe. What if one day she missed the bus? Or got lost in the big school. How would she know what rooms to go into? They had different rooms for each subject, Kathleen said. And what was a subject? They only got lessons in their school. You got the belt if you forgot your gym things. She didn't have gym things. What would she do about that? Her sandshoes were for wearing. You could get thirds of school dinners, Kathleen said. That was good. She'd take thirds. As long as they didn't make you eat mashed turnip or broth or boiled cabbage. Marjie nearly choked as her mind tasted the cooked vegetables. The gym teacher was a woman, but she looked like a man. Her mind gave her a strange picture there. The men she knew sometimes had bristles on their faces when they needed to shave. Some, like her father, had tattoos on their forearms, anchors or thistles and words like 'Mother', in blue ink. They wore thigh waders going to their boats and carried their creels on their shoulders. On Sunday their faces were smooth and they wore their suits and ties and polished shoes to go to church. She didn't see how a woman gym teacher could look like any of that. She wore a divided skirt and you could see her legs. Marjie never saw big people's legs, only the bits that their skirts didn't cover. The men mightn't have any legs for all that she knew. But they must have because they wore boots. Only those she played with had legs like that. She'd see plenty when she went into the sea. Far out of the village they'd go, to the empty places by the cliffs, and there they'd strip to their vest and jump in. Once her mother had nearly killed her for running away with little Paul's nappy pin to fasten her vest between her legs. She didn't do it again. The big ones sat up the back of the bus. If you took their seat you were for it. Marjie thought she would look for an empty seat far from the big ones and just look out the bus window. She wouldn't say a word to anyone then no-one could say anything to her.

"How are you not playing football?" She didn't hear nor see Duncan until he was on her.

"Because," Marjie said, swinging her legs out and in. Through the wooden wall of the shed Jeannie's tongue still rattled on.

"Anyway," Duncan said, "I'm going to make a banjo."

"How?" Marjie asked and she wished he would take his freckly face away from her.

"It's easy," she thought that if he wouldn't be still he would blow up in front of her. "Guess what I found at the midden?"

"I don't know," she said, hoping that her disinterest would send him some place else.

"Well, if you want to know, I found a shortbread tin."

Marjie looked at him, failing completely to see what he was driving at.

"It's round," he explained. "It's in the lobby. Are you wanting to see it?"

Marjie gave up. There'd be no peace for her with Duncan like this. "Alright," she said and jumped down from the dyke.

Not only had he a round red tartan base from a shortbread tin, he also had his father's claw hammer and a pocketful of his four inch nails. And from somewhere he had picked up a length of white wood about two feet long and two inches in breadth.

"You can easy make a banjo," he said to Marjie when both they and the materials were spread on the dyke again.

Marjie said nothing.

"Right, this is how you do it," he said, the hair on the crown of his head sprouting like the top of a pineapple. He put two nails between his teeth and lined up his wood to his tin. "Right, keep that," he said and he selected one of the nails and lifted the hammer.

"Keep it, I said," he said to Marjie as she shied away from his swipe.

"I'm keeping it. Watch my hand," and she screwed her face tight at the expected pain.

He hammered the nail through the inside edge of the tin, trying to catch the wood with it when it came through. It was a harder job than he had first thought. It was very awkward working that way. First the hammer head struck the tip of the nail's head and caught Marjie's wrist.

"Ow," she cried. "My hand's in bits with you."

"Can you not hold the thing right?" he said and he swung again. The second blow drove the nail through the metal, the point of it catching the wood. With short rapid blows he drove the best part of the nail in.

"Look at that then," he held it up for Marjie's inspection. "Now for the next one," and he took the other nail from his mouth.

"How many are you putting in to it?" Marjie asked, thinking of her hand.

"I don't know," he said. "Three maybe. It'll need to hold."

"Well, it's not holding very good like that," she said.

His base dangled loosely from its neck.

"Are you ready then?" he asked.

"Right," she said, and she squeezed her eyes shut.

It was even more difficult this time. The first nail he anchored in the centre of the wood, where the circle and straight line met. The nails to either side of it had a gap to bridge. Getting them through the tin was easy, securing them in the wood was impossible for him. He tried pushing his wood to meet the nail's sharp point, but it twisted away from it. He huffed and he puffed and he had the tin nearly flattened. But the nails shone through, impaling only the air. He used the claw end of the hammer and pulled them free, to discard them at his side. He took more from his pocket and began again. His success was no better. He tried a different approach by going in through the side of the wood and catching the tin. None of it worked and there was a mound of bent nails beside him.

"Dash it," he said. "That was a good tin. I could've made something out of that tin."

"You better hide that nails," Marjie said, glad that that was over. She never knew with Duncan. "I don't think you can make banjoes from tins."

"I know," he said, and he put the bent nails into his trouser pocket. "I was just wanting one."

T E N

"The first thing we do," Dougal Innes said to Marjie on Monday morning, "is to bag the rolls."

She looked up at him and waited for him to say more.

"This book here," he said, and he reached below the counter for a small book with a blue cover.

"Look," he showed her. "Beulah takes four, your mother has ten, that ones are all sixes." He drew a dirty finger nail through the names. "And don't forget the farm. She doesn't come in till we close. And write the names on this bags here," he brought his hand down onto a pile of brown paper bags on the counter. "If someone comes in for two use that bags," and he pointed to a white pile.

Marjie understood. She was to take the rolls from the wooden tray and put them into the bags, then mark them off in the book. It was easy. The rolls that were left were to be sold.

Her day hadn't long begun when she found her first mistake. Her pencil made holes in the bags when she tried to write the names over the rolls.

"Write their names on first," Dougal Innes said as he leant over her, a slice of corned beef in the centre of a fresh roll in his hand. "It's easier that way," and he tore the roll with his fingers and put the piece into his mouth. He looked up as the door opened. Poor Benny was first into the shop that morning. "Serve Benny," he said. "I'll do this for you," and he squashed the fresh rolls as he gripped the bags in one hand and used his pen with the other.

"I'll take four rolls," Poor Benny's face beamed at her.

"Are they ordered?" Marjie asked him.

"I'll take four rolls," he said as if she hadn't heard.

"Benny's rolls are ordered," Dougal Innes handed her a bag. "They're under Beulah's name," he said.

"And the sugar," the words came with difficulty from his slack mouth.

"How much sugar are you wanting?" Marjie was aware of Dougal Innes standing beside her. She wished someone would come for stamps.

"The sugar," Benny continued to smile.

"Is Beulah at the jam?" Dougal Innes asked him.

Poor Benny's smile widened. "The jam," he told Marjie.

"Give him six pounds," Dougal Innes said, and Poor Benny nodded his head and wouldn't stop.

Marjie had no idea what six pounds of sugar looked like. She scooped some from the big bag on the floor into her brown paper one, she carried it over to the scales. The hand was nowhere near the six. She did it again and the hand was nearly there. The third time it was nearer to the eight. Back she went to the big bag and poured the surplus, or what she judged was surplus, back into it. By the time she had finished with Poor Benny she was spent, and only a quarter of an hour had passed since Dougal

Innes came to unlock his door.

It was that way until after eleven. Then things began to ease up a little.

"Take something for yourself," Dougal Innes said, and he disappeared into the back of the shop to count packets of soap powder. He had spent most of the morning up until then in the Post Office, giving Marjie the time to find her way. As she devoured a macaroon bar she could hear him speaking to the Oxydol.

"Ay Marjie," Duncan burst through the door, doing his best to separate it from its hinges. "How are you getting on?"

His face had had its usual cat's lick, the tide mark beneath his chin was there for anybody to see.

"What are you doing here?" Marjie hissed at him, nearly choking on a snowball.

"Came to see you," he said, his grin spread across his face.

Marjie wished he hadn't. She didn't want Duncan, or any of them coming into the shop when she was there.

"Anyway I got sent for the messages," he said, and he looked about him as if he had never seen the inside of the place. He walked over to the 'Breeze Soap' placard and stood before it, studying it and mouthing the words on it.

"You know fine that's 'Breeze'," Marjie said to him. "Give me the note." She wished that he would go before anyone came in. She got into a state if more than one was waiting to be served.

"Rich Tea," he spoke aloud as he studied the metal placard beside the door, and looked at the boy holding out a biscuit to a parrot on a perch. If he had a biscuit it's not to a parrot he would give it.

"Hurry up," Marjie said. "Someone might come in."

He walked to the counter and handed her the crumpled piece of paper with their mother's writing on it. While she read it he began to attack the base of the counter with his sandshoe. Then he spread himself over the counter and picked at some imaginary thing there with his fingernail. His shirt was buttoned high to his neck, his stockings were pulled straight to his knee, he must have taken someone's garters, and he looked hot.

"Ma said I've to get an ice lolly," he said without looking up.

"We've none till Thursday," Marjie said and she put a packet of Brooke Bond tea beside the loaves and the rolls.

He left the counter and walked over to the door again.

"I've to get an ice lolly," he looked away from the boy on the placard.

"Give me the bag," Marjie said. "We haven't any ice lollies, I told you. They'll be in on Thursday," and she snatched the bag from him, flattening her mother's rolls below a large tin of syrup. She was glad her mother was still taking Brooke Bond tea. Another three labels after this packet, and the headress was hers.

"Are you wanting liquorice pipes then?" she pushed the bag to Duncan.

"No," and he resumed his kicking of the counter.

"Well, what then? Hurry up," she tried to be polite when the door opened and a little wifie with a bent back came in.

"I don't know," he said. "How much are the penny caramels?"

"You're very funny," Marjie said, her tone telling him that he was everything but, and she thrust the bag at him, taking the teasing grin from his face and nearly his front teeth as well.

"Take that note back to Ma," she said and opened the big brown book.

"Give me a lucky bag then and a sherbert dab," he said. The bag in the face had shaken the cockiness from him.

Marjie would have handed the entire shop and its contents to him just to be able to see him going through the door. The old wifie jumped when he nearly took the door after him. She looked at the closed door for some seconds.

"He's in a hurry to be off playing at something," she said, a smile in her eyes. "Have you a black reel, maital?" and she counted pennies from her purse.

After that it was quiet again and Marjie built a pyramid in the window from the Brooke Bond tea. Dougal Innes stopped counting things in his store and stepped through to the Post Office. On the way he commended Marjie on her initiative and said that she was a good help to him. Marjie took another macaroon bar when she heard him saying, "Yes, speaking." She was wondering if she could squeeze a small pyramid of 'Snow Fire' to one side of the tea when Jeannie came, trailing little Dan and little Paul along with her.

"What are you lot wanting?" she barked at them.

"We came to see you," Jeannie said. She'd started parting her hair on the side and had two of her mother's kirby grips holding her dosan clear of her forehead.

"We're wanting sweeties," little Dan said, his jumper like a second skin to him.

"Have you money?" Marjie asked.

"You can give us them," little Dan said.

"I cannot," Marjie spoke slowly to the three. "I'll get into trouble for that. If you haven't money you can't get anything."

Little Dan looked to Jeannie. "You said," accusation rang from him. "You said Marjie would give us anything we were wanting."

"Well, I will not," Marjie said and little Paul started his crying. Little Dan's bottom lip quivered dangerously and Jeannie wished she had never told them she would take them to the shop.

"It's alright," she tried to soothe. "We'll come back. We'll get pennies and we'll come back." Little Dan looked at her and wondered if he would trust her again so soon. Little Paul wouldn't be comforted.

Marjie weighed up the situation. If little Paul's howling didn't bring Dougal Innes from his phone, then she'd likely get away with it.

"Here you are. Now get," and she thrust a liquorice pipe to each. "And don't come back without any money."

Jeannie was glad to be rescued. She pushed them through the door before her, little Paul's black mouth still bubbling.

Marjie sat on the box of Carnation Milk. She hoped they weren't going to come in every day.

Summer girls in pretty dresses came. They bounced into the shop looking for good things for picnics, the sun in their mouths and in their hair.

"Are you working for the WHOLE holidays?" they asked and their laughter carried back to Marjie as they went along the street.

She didn't care. She wasn't like them anyway. They giggled at nothing.

And those needing to use the phone came.

"I haven't one lump of coal left," a woman said.

"Oh?" Marjie was sad about that, but didn't know what else she should be.

"I've been without since the weekend," she said.

"Oh," Marjie said again and hoped her sympathy showed through her vacant expression.

"I'll need you to phone for me," the woman went on.

"Eh?" Marjie said and nearly choked on the coconut from the macaroon.

"Will you phone over to Balmore for me like a good girl," her purse was gripped in her hand.

"I don't know," Marjie's attention was focused now as she tried to quietly overcome the effects of the coconut.

"Come now till I tell you," the woman said. Marjie followed her to the kiosk and tried to clear the tears from her eyes.

"Who is it you're wanting me to phone?" she spoke loudly because the woman was older than her mother. With the two of them inside the kiosk and the door closed the woman was nearly on top of her. There was a smell of mothballs from her and Marjie thought that she was going to pass out.

"I'm asking you to phone over to Nancy for me. At the Post Office. I want you to ask her if the coal man came in yet. The whole place is waiting, you know."

Marjie didn't. She thought it was only themselves that ever had no coal.

Marjie wasn't yolach with the phone. She stood there, the woman squeezed to her back and read what was written on the board above.

"Never mind that," the woman said. "I'll keep you right," and she opened her purse and handed some coppers to her. The smell from the mothballs was getting stronger. She likely wore her good coat to come out. Marjie wished the woman would go outside or at least leave the door open.

"Do you know her number?" Marjie asked. The mothballs were hard to take after nearly choking on coconut.

"Oh, I don't have a number," she sounded surprised, as if she'd been asked could she fly an aeroplane. "Just say it's me and I'm asking Nancy if the coal has arrived. Say that. Has the coal arrived? Tell her the whole place is waiting."

None of it made sense to Marjie. How was she supposed to get someone who would put her in touch with Nancy when there wasn't a number between them. In the end the woman saw this too. "I'll come up when Dougal's back," she said and bored through the door of the kiosk, letting it fly back in Marjie's face. Marjie was glad to be freed, distanced from the stench of the mothballs.

"I'll come back," the woman said again. "How long do you think Dougal'll be?"

"Not long," Marjie was glad to say. "He just went up to his house." She saw no need to mention that that was nearly an hour ago.

"I'll come later," the woman said and she walked westwards.

Marjie watched her going. She could have walked to Balmore and found out about the coal in the time she was nearly crushing her to a mothbally death in the kiosk. And she'd be back. Marjie lifted the flap and went behind the counter to wait. She'd take a pineapple chew. They lasted a long time.

"You can go now," Dougal Innes said around half past five. "I'll see to herself from the farm. We'll not see anyone much more now." He knew his customers and they'd all been in.

"O.K. then," Marjie was quick through the flap.

"You did well for your first day," he said from the slicing machine. He lifted the bacon from it onto a white enamel tray then took the cloth from the side of the machine and began to wipe pieces of bacon and boiled ham from the blades. He told her that he would do any slicing until she got the hang of it. She was glad about that. She wondered if she would ever get the hang of the thing.

She walked on air to her house. "Ay, Beulah," she waved to Poor Benny's sister picking the rhubarb for the jam. Beulah straightened her back to see who was speaking.

"Is that it then, Marjie maital?" Beulah said and buried her head among the leaves once more.

Marjie was in a hurry to be home. She felt good, she was a worker now, helping with the upkeep of the house. Her heart quickened a little when she thought of her books. She hadn't thought of them the whole day. Nobody better have found them. She hadn't had the chance to open them yet even.

The smell of someone's supper came through an open back window of one of the houses on the shore street. She wondered what her mother had on.

She stopped at the shed. Her father was still in there. All her life it seemed she had watched those hands at work, creating something out of very little.

"Is it hard to do that?" she had asked him once. Long ago her eye had given up trying to follow the speed of the needle and the string.

"No, not hard at all," he had replied. "Watch what I'm doing here," and he had showed her the needle and the string. "In there, see," he held the square of the net before her. "Hold it like that." It was no use. She still couldn't follow. "It's just like knitting," he had said.

Knitting a net. She shook her head. She couldn't knit either.

"Like this," the teacher said. Marjie's ball of pale blue wool was grey through use and abuse. "In," the teacher stressed, and she pushed the red plastic needle through a black loop. "Over," she said and she looped the wool around the working needle. "Through," and she hooked the wool through. "And off," there was triumph in the teacher's voice as she transferred the loop onto the other needle. "Now you do it."

Marjie had looked at the teacher then, her face full of completely nothing. "Please miss, I don't know how," she said.

"How did it go then," her father asked, his eye to the net.

"It was no bother," she said. "I never got to work the bacon slicer the day. He said I can when I learn. Do you know this? Jimmy's wife marks."

His hands stopped their work and he looked at her. "Now I don't want to hear any of that kind of talk," he warned her. "What people do is their own affair," and his look was long and it went in on her.

She looked from him to the ground.

"Tell your mother I'll be shortly," he said, his eye back with the needle.

"What's in it?" she asked her mother as soon as she walked through the door.

"It's there," her mother had the food ready and keeping warm on the fender. She was sitting in her chair. The summer heat was hard for her to stand. Sometimes it was hard for her to stand herself.

Marjie lifted her plate.

"Mind, it'll be hot," her mother said. "Take the towel," and she pulled it from the rail. "Did you have a lot in?" she asked as Marjie walked to the sofa and put her plate on its arm.

"Well, we were busy in the morning," she spoke

through a mouthful of fried potato. "There's always a rush on the rolls and the visitors like their bacon. This is good bacon," she chewed a piece.

"Did everyone pay?" her mother asked.

"Except us," Marjie said. There would be little to be gained by telling about Jimmy's wife and more besides. "Nobody west the town has coal," she added.

"Well, they'll get it in the morning. That's not long," her mother said and turned Colin's and her father's plates around.

"My Da said to tell you he'll be coming."

"You know your father could have come in when this was ready."

"Where did all the rest go?" Marjie asked.

"They're not far," her mother said.

"Did they get their supper?"

"Swallowed it whole," her mother's voice sounded tired. "Your father starts work on Monday."

"Where?"

"On the new road."

"Oh," Marjie said, completely clueless as to where the new road lay.

"Your father's getting the workman's bus."

"Is he?"

"Well," her mother said. "There is no-one else who drives or can do work on the engine if it needs it."

"Ay," Marjie said. "Dougal Innes and the big boys were laughing about what he has on the top shelf."

"Jimmy the Soldier got a television, Dan," Jeannie said as they picked the buttercups which grew around the well.

"I don't know a television," little Dan said, pulling them by their heads.

"You're awful daft, Dan. Anybody knows that," Jeannie told him and yowled when the nettle in her bunch stung.

Little Dan thought as he pulled the yellow heads. Jeannie would laugh if he said what he was thinking.

"Jimmy the Soldier's going to be the first to get one," she said.

Little Dan thought some more. Then he said it anyway. "What do you do with one?" he asked.

Jeannie stopped her picking. "You don't do anything," she said. "Televisions have stuff on them."

"What kind of stuff," he stood beside her.

"I don't know what stuff, Dan. Just stuff and that."

"Is the stuff on the top?"

Jeannie rolled her eyes to the blue sky. How could she tell Dan what she didn't know herself, and still make him believe.

"The stuff is on it," she tried again.

"Is the stuff a horse?" he asked catching sight of Jocky on his lookout.

"I don't know," she said and she caught her top lip with her bottom teeth and put her face against his. "He's just getting it anyway," she said.

Little Dan was brave. He thought even more. After a while he spoke.

"Who's giving it to him?" he asked.

"The man on the carrier. He'll give you anything. He

gave Peg a mat," Jeannie said, and she picked her buttercup from the root. She was beginning to be tired with Dan and his questions.

"Jimmy the Soldier hasn't a Ma," little Dan said.

Jeannie said nothing to that and went on searching for tall buttercups.

"How has Jimmy the Soldier not got a Ma, Jeannie," he persisted.

"Because," Jeannie told him. "Big people don't have Mas, Dan."

"How?"

"Because."

"Has he got a Da, Jeannie?" Little Dan's grip on his bunch was so firm that his hand was wet with the juice.

"Jimmy the Soldier lives on his lone, Dan," Jeannie explained.

Little Dan thought about that. "If I was living on my lone I would be wanting Ma and Da, would you Jeannie?"

"Yes, Dan," she said and they looked at one another. "But you could have your bed for yourself."

"You could eat lots of dinner," little Dan said. "I don't know where Jimmy the Soldier's Ma and Da is Jeannie."

"They're away," Jeannie informed him. "It's only when you're little you have them."

"Is our Ma and Da going to go away, Jeannie?"

"I don't know. Likely."

Little Dan thought about that. Then his face appeared to crumple from the inside, his mouth opened wide and he squeezed the water from his eyes.

"You're always at the bagpipes, Dan," Jeannie said and she buried her nose in her fistful of gold.

Marjie was glad when a quarter to one on Wednesday afternoon came. She had only been in the shop for two and half days and it was beginning to feel like long enough. It was still bright outside. Kathleen had come for her mother's messages in the morning and told her she'd be along to call for her after dinner. Marjie could barely wait to be about with her own age again. She felt so good that she even agreed to go into the goals for Duncan. When she didn't let the ball pass her once she knew she couldn't go wrong. And when she heard Duncan singing her praises, her head swelled like the football. "Marjie's great in goals, isn't she boys?" She took their cheers as her due.

"Did Kathleen come yet?" she asked her mother when she was back in the house.

"There's been no-one," her mother said. "Mind your feet," and she swept the brush across the linoleum.

Marjie was getting tired of waiting for Kathleen. She jumped from the dyke and walked into the middle of the road and looked along it. The road was empty. No-one was out for the shop on the halfday. If Kathleen didn't come soon she was off.

From the shore street she could hear the voices of Duncan and the rest of the teams. She climbed back up onto the dyke and stood there for a better view of anyone coming. There was still no sign of anybody. She gave a big jump and landed nearly into the middle of the road. The voices pulled her down the vennel opposite and along the shore street to Ian Ross's house.

"What are you going to do?" Marjie bounded up to the group.

"What's to do in this place," Ian Ross sounded disgusted.

"Will we raid the orchard?" Jeannie was bold in company.

"I can't be bothered walking all that way," Duncan was picking flaking skin from his nose. "I'm nearly dead after that game."

"Well, is anyone coming to jump the channel?" ventured Marjie.

"No," their voices came as one as they set their faces against her.

"Well, I just thought," she said.

"And you know what thought did," she never knew Ian Ross could be cheeky like that.

"Well, I don't know then," she defended herself, and she pulled the top from one of Ian Ross's mother's lupins which rose above the paling.

"We could raid the orchard," Arthur Morrison had followed them from the park.

"We said we're not doing that," Duncan was short with him.

"We'll go and watch Jimmy the Soldier's television?" No-one had noticed Kathleen's coming. "I just thought," she said when nobody spoke. Wordlessly they turned to one another, silently the unanimous decision was taken.

"Ay, come on boys," Duncan spoke for all of them.

"Ay, come on," Ian Ross said and the pack moved from his door to one further along that street.

There wasn't much of a garden below Jimmy the Soldier's window, just one or two flowers and a rose bush to make the place look nice. Like all the gardens in the street his main one was on the other side of the through-way and ran down to the shore.

"I can't see anything," Jeannie spoke to the middle of Duncan's back. The big boys were at the front, the girls and little Dan were elbowed to the back.

"No-one can see anything," Duncan answered her, his feet trampling on Jimmy the Soldier's marigolds as he peered through the top pane.

"He hasn't got it on," Ian Ross said, and his eyes scanned the large cabinet with the small grey screen in the fireside corner of the Soldier's sitting room.

"Stop shoving," Arthur Morrison spittled to those at the back as they pushed him deeper into the roses.

"Is he in?" Duncan asked Ian Ross.

"If he is I'm not seeing him. There's not a soul in there."

"We're not seeing anything here," Marjie said and she stood on top of Arthur Morrison's sandal.

"Be quiet, will you. We're looking," Duncan said. "He's not in and he doesn't have it on."

Ian Ross gave a small leap. "He is. There's him," as a figure walked through a door into the room.

Jimmy the Soldier, who used to be a soldier, stood in the centre of his living room, looking out at those who were looking in.

"Can we watch your television?" Duncan raised his voice.

"Put it on," pleaded Ian Ross.

"We're not seeing nothing," Jeannie was doing her

best to scrape the skin from Marjie's heels.

"What's happening?" Kathleen asked.

"The next one that pushes me is for it," Arthur Morrison's jumper was stuck to the rose bush.

"Ach, come on man, please," Duncan wheedled to the silent Soldier.

Jimmy the Soldier walked across to his window.

"He's going to say something boys," Duncan reported back.

The Soldier lifted the bottom half. He said something.

"Bugger off," they watched his mouth. "And if I catch any of you back here I'll take the skin from your arses," and he slammed his window with a bang.

Ian Ross was a tall, elegant looking boy. He let some elegant phrases fall from his mouth. "Big bugger," he spewed. "Big old bugger." That Jimmy the Soldier weighed less than ten stone and was younger than anyone's father didn't seem to apply.

Arthur Morrison ripped himself from the thorns and took up his fighting stance clear of the window, the largest stone he could find in his raised hand he frightened the glass. When he realised that no one was seeing him he let his arm and the stone drop and trailed after the departing party.

"What are we going to do now?" Duncan asked Ian Ross once they were back on his mother's doorstep.

Ian Ross put his hand up to Duncan's ear and spoke behind it.

"Ay, O.K." Duncan was furtive as they went together. Little Dan followed.

"Where are you two off to?" Marjie called out to them.

"Mind your own business," Duncan said without turning his head. "And keep him. He's not coming with us," he swung to say.

Little Dan kept going. Duncan stopped. "Did you hear what I said?" His voice was becoming louder with each word. "Keep him. Get," he said to little Dan. "You needn't think you're coming with us."

Marjie went to little Dan. "Come on Dan. Come on," she pulled at his jumper sleeve. "You're going to smoke," she flung at Duncan. "I'm telling."

"Shut up you," his face was red beneath his freckles. "Just you do and see what you get," and he punched her on the arm.

"Ow, that was sore," Marjie rubbed at the pain.

"It was meant to be," he said, and he walked away, laughing something to Ian Ross who pushed back at him with his shoulder.

"Come on Dan," she said and she tugged at little Dan once more. Little Dan was sitting in the middle of the road and didn't want to come anywhere.

"Come on Dan," Marjie said. "Get up," and she tried to lift him.

Kathleen was practising her dancing steps over at Ian Ross's gable end, her frock flying from her long slim legs when she birled around.

"Are you coming up to the barley?" Marjie looked from little Dan to the pair of strong legs before her.

"Eh?" she said.

"Up to the barley field," Arthur Morrison said. Marjie didn't know what to say. Her only thought previously was to get little Dan off the road. She looked at Arthur Morrison's face, to his loose mouth which dribbled his words from it, to the enlarged eyes behind his glasses. He was an only child whose father went out to work one day and didn't come back. His mother called him 'Our Arthur' and made curls in his fair hair.

His big face looked back at her and smiled and she was afraid of something she didn't know about.

"I'm telling on you Arthur Morrison," her words came quickly as she used all her strength to move little Dan. "I'm just telling," she turned back to warn as she pulled little Dan along after her.

"I'm going now," she told Kathleen.

"Already?" Kathleen asked as she stopped her pirouetting.

"Dan's wanting home," she lied.

"I'm not," Dan told Kathleen.

"You're going," Marjie said.

"He can go by himself, can't you Dan?" Kathleen said.

"Ay," little Dan said.

"Well, I'm taking him," Marjie said and caught his cuff. She didn't want to hear anyone's argument. Arthur Morrison was still there and he was looking. "You can do what you like," she flung at little Dan and she raced away from there.

As she sat on the dyke and watched little Dan emerging from the vennel she faced a new thing in her life. She had always disliked Arthur Morrison. Anybody would. He threw the biggest stones he could find at whoever passed his mother's gate. And her fear of him came from what the stones might do to her. But today that fear had another shape. And she didn't know what name to put on it.

She was afraid of many things. But these were all tangible. She was afraid of her mother's hand but she was quick and knew how to dodge. That was built in to her. She was afraid of Grace's hand but Grace's blows weren't too hard. She was afraid of Colin's hand if he so much as caught her even looking at his bike. She was afraid for her mother sometimes. All these fears she knew, they were never far from her. But what she feared in Arthur Morrison was perhaps the strongest fear of all and she had no idea where it came from. To say that what she was feeling was a sense of menace, of threat wouldn't have made any sense to Marjie, for these words were not in her vocabulary.

E L E V E N

The summer holidays which had promised to last forever on that first day were hurrying to their end. They had done everything. They swam too much, took too much of the sun, they crammed their bellies with far too many hard apples and pears from the orchard and paid for it for too long a time afterwards. Too many times they knocked on The Soldier's front window and too often they felt the weight from a demented mother's hand when they trailed the shore over her newly washed linoleum or good mats or both. And they fought amongst themselves too many times altogether. Except Marjie.

For Marjie wanted to be away from the shop and if school was the price she'd be willing to pay it. The novelty of being a wage earner had long worn off. She wanted to be out and running with the rest of them. The shop was alright when it rained, but it didn't rain much that summer. And she'd never touch another macaroon bar in her life. Just thinking about putting her teeth into one made her want to spew. Her wage, which had seemed so large to her before she had to work for it, seemed like nothing much at all when she handed it to her mother and received a two shilling bit for herself. All that she had to show for that summer was a packet of shampoo which she put in the bottom of her father's toolbox so that Colin wouldn't take it. The rest of her money went to the ice cream man on Saturday night.

As the days wore on she thought more about the new school.

On the Saturday before school restarted Cis put her good coat and shoes on, dusted some powder over her face and told Jeannie and John Clark to keep their eye on little Dan and little Paul. Then she walked over to the end of the road to catch the eleven o'clock bus into the town. At a quarter to one o'clock Marjie took pies home for their dinner and their father made a pot of tea. Marjie wasn't going back to the shop that afternoon. The holidaymakers had left the village and with most of the locals having been in in the morning Dougal Innes told Marjie she could have the rest of the day for herself. And he had paid her for the full week.

"When will Ma come back?" Little Dan would only eat the pastry from his pie.

"I'm wanting my Ma," little Paul began to cry. He didn't like any of the pie.

"Your Mammy'll be soon," his father spoke softly to him. "Be a good boy now. Eat your food pet, don't spit it like that."

"You can watch them now," Jeannie spoke to Marjie. She liked pies and would eat whatever anyone didn't want. "I watched them all morning."

"I'm not watching them," Marjie said. "They can play out."

"How?" Jeannie asked. "What are you going to do?"

"Something. I'm not telling you. But they're not staying in." She looked at the two. In they'd be everywhere. They were never still.

"Well, you can do what you like," their father told them. "I've things to do." He put his empty mug on the table. "We'd best keep a bit fire on for your mother," and he shovelled coal from the pail onto the embers.

With the house to herself Marjie sat in the big chair and thought. She was only up to page four of *Silver Chief*. She could do that. In the peace, with the quiet around her. As soon as the still protesting Jeannie and her two charges were through she bounded to the dresser and raked below the jumpers for her book. Draped across the big chair she read yet again what it said on the label inside. First Prize awarded to Marjory E. Clark. She thought on Marjory E. Clark. She didn't know her well, she was some person distant to herself. Herself someplace else. At her beginning. Or in the schoolroom. The teacher always called her Marjory and it was as Marjory that she would answer. But out of the school, even at Sunday School, she was Marjie. And to everyone in the villages she was Marjie. Marjie who wouldn't walk where she could run, Marjie whose face was forever smiling to those outside of her own home, Marjie who would fly for a message for a neighbour if she thought that there might be a threepenny bit in it for her. And there was the Marjie who was about the shore and the rocks from the time that she could walk.

She turned to page four and began to read. And as she read Jack London's words she heard her mother's voice. 'Books', her mother was tired with her. 'Your head is never out of them. I'll give you reading my girl'. She closed the book and put it back among the jumpers.

She didn't mean to upset her mother. It was just that she couldn't stop herself reading. She'd read anything that had writing on it. Even the labels on the sauce bottles or the box of matches. She knew how to make cremola custard because she read that packet. When Colin reached the secondary school she'd help him with his spellings. She was seven then.

Marjie decided that she would wash the floor for her mother. Surely that would make her mother pleased with her. She pulled her cuff over her hand and lifted the kettle. She shook it and felt the water in it. There was enough. Then she went ben to the backplace for the floorcloth, the scrubber and the packet of Rinso. She poured too much Rinso into the basin and left it there because she didn't know what else to do. She wondered where she would start. She pulled the chair away from the bed and knelt. Backwards and forth she pulled the scrubber. Round in circles she took it and covered the floor in soap. The linoleum was dirty. The patch she'd washed was the colour of the sand, the rest was the colour of the earth from all the feet and she'd never get her knees clean. She put the chair back and started along the front of the dresser. She pushed the brush forwards with both hands, driving it to do its work. Already the water was cooling to slime. Three times she rinsed out the floorcloth before she was able to remove all the soap. It put more down than it lifted off. It was good that she was strong. Her belly ached with pushing the big chairs and her hair annoyed her face. She thought of taking up the mat in front of the fire, but then decided to wash around it. That way she'd be done quicker and then there was always the water. By the time she had moved and scrubbed under the table she was melting and was so tired that she nearly rattled the sugar bowl onto the floor. She looked to what was left to be done. Just the square from the bottom of the bed to the door. She added the rest of the water in the kettle to the grey slime. She had no idea of time, of how long she'd been on her knees. She was just getting into her stride with the warmer water when the light coming through the open door disappeared.

"What do you think you're doing," her mother's voice said, and she flung her parcels onto the bed. She marched over to the fireplace and lifted the kettle. "You've used all my water," she said and she banged the kettle down and made for Marjie. "That'll teach you, my girl," and her hand lashed out.

"There's no need for that. Leave the bairn alone. She was only doing her best." Her father had come up the path with her mother. His voice was tired as he stood in the centre of the room and looked at Cis.

She wheeled towards him. "Where are that bairns?" he heard the accusation from her.

"The bairns are fine. Peg has them picking her pea-pods."

"I only had that bit to do," Marjie had sought refuge on the fender. She began to cry and two dirty circles looked from her knees.

"Using all the water," her mother's voice was still high. "Get me that packet of Rinso till I see what you used."

"I never used hardly anything," Marjie sobbed, her dirty fists rubbing the tears from her eyes.

Her mother caught up the basin and walked through the closet door with it.

"Never you mind," her father said, and he put his hand on her head.

"I was only trying to help," she said.

"I know that. I know that fine. Dry your face now. Don't say anything for the sake of your mother." He clamped his lips and shook his head. "You know the way it is with her," and he went out. The years had been hard on John Clark. There was a stoop to him now, and his clothes hung around his spare frame.

"You've used all my Rinso with your carry on," her mother waved the half empty packet in front of Marjie, then put it on the mantelpiece. "You can get yourself to the well."

Marjie rose from the fender and walked from the room. For once there was nothing left in her with which to challenge her mother's injustice.

"And then you can find that bairns for me," her mother called after her.

Cis sat in her chair with her coat on. She didn't have the energy to remove it. She spread her arms along the chair's arms and looked ahead of her. She saw nothing, no sound came in on her. That old witch in the tearoom had put her wrong. She'd only gone in for a sit down until it was time for the bus. And who would be sitting there. Some family! Where she came from, family didn't treat people like this. Where she came from, family helped when people needed it. And you didn't have to ask. They saw how things were with one another.

"It's yourself that's in it," she knew that sleekit way of hers. "I didn't think to see you in here, what with John being out of work. He's been idle a long time. But you have your family to keep you. The poor bairns are growing. Is Grace left the school yet?"

But she had been fit for her. "No, Grace hasn't left the school yet missus," she said. "And it may interest you to know that John is not out of work."

The old witch would have the last word on her though. "Och," she laughed. "John'll soon not need to bother with work when they all take a pay home." Her eyes were everywhere, looking at the parcels. If she hadn't been feeling so bad she'd have told that one where to get off. Her who'd never had a man or a bairn in her life. Not having anyone to consider but herself. What did she know about what it was like? Looking at her, Cis thanked God that she was different. If she thought she'd end up like that she'd die. She started on John the minute she got off the bus. Told him all about his beautiful aunt.

"You pay too much mind to people," he told her and she wouldn't hand him the parcels. "You know what that one's like. She's ever been that way. Never mind her."

And she hadn't a halfpenny left. Everything cost more than she would have thought. She'd have to hide again from the shilling-a-week man. Thinking that way, her thought grew resentful. Maybe the old witch was right. He was working now, but when the job was done, what then? He'd have his fags though. Smoking himself to death. Lines and lobster pots, lines and lobster pots. She was sick of the sea, sick of it all. My, if them at home could see her now.

It wasn't her mother's hand that had sent Marjie crying on the fender. A skelp wouldn't do that. She was at home with harshness. It was the kindness in her father's voice that was the undoing of her. When he had said 'never you mind' that way, she was his little lassie once more. But there were things growing in her that stopped her being the bairn she was, the bairn that wanted to climb up into his lap, and so she hung her head and cried. She cried because she wasn't the little one and she cried for her mother to reach out to her and because she knew that she never would and she cried because she didn't know why she was crying, and she cried because her tender heart was in two.

"You're a big help to your mother," Mrs MacIntyre always said the same thing. Marjie looked at her, but didn't stop. Mrs MacIntyre was always pinning out a dishcloth.

"Ay," Marjie hoped that their neighbour wouldn't see her tear streaked face.

"That's your water," she was huffy with her mother when she returned. The floor looked daft, with the black square at the door. She could easily have finished it.

"Get me the parcels," her mother hadn't moved since she left.

"All of them?"

"You can leave the biggest one," her mother said. She sounded like herself again.

Her mother pulled the string from the brown paper and tore the paper away. "This is your blazer," she said and she held it before Marjie. "Try it on."

"It fits fine," Marjie said and her hand caressed the gold braid on the lapel. "The sleeves are just right too," and she put out her arm for her mother to see.

"It fits lovely," her mother's face was soft. "The badge

is in one of the pockets. I'll sew it on the night. Take it off now. I don't want you getting it dirty."

"Can I go and show Da?" the light shone through the dirt on Marjie's face.

"You can show him when he comes in," her mother said.

"Is that my tie?" Marjie made a grab for it from her mother's hand.

"You know your hands are filthy," her mother said and she gave her the tie.

"What else did I get?"

"There's a navy skirt and two white blouses and two vests and pairs of knickers here." She clapped the small parcel. "This is your shoes. Try the skirt on."

Marjie didn't know what to say. The only time they got new clothes was when her mother got the grant for them. But that was to be shared among all who attended school. The most each got was shoes and a jumper. Then there was the Red Cross clothes, but she wouldn't think about that. Most of her life she wore other people's clothes, walked in somebody else's shoes that hurt her feet. Now, suddenly, all this. Everything.

"Where did you get the money?" she asked her mother as she tried to rip her frock over her head in her hurry to have the new skirt on.

"It's yours," her mother said. "It's what you worked for. I bet you thought that I'd spent it," her mother said.

"No, I never," Marjie's protest was too loud. "Is my skirt O.K.?"

"Turn around," her mother said.

Marjie obeyed.

"Let me see the waist," her mother said and Marjie stood in front of her. Her mother put her hand inside the front waistband.

"Is that tight?" she asked.

"No, there's heaps of room. Look," and she pulled the waistband away from herself to show her mother how much.

"You wouldn't have the tea ready?" John Clark looked around the door. "My throat's that dry," the teasing light was in his eyes for them.

"Come in," Cis said. "Fill the kettle for me," and she handed it to him.

"Look at all I got," Marjie halted him as he was about to go through the door. "Look," and she held the blazer up for his inspection.

"Well, see you look after them," the kettle hung uselessly from his hand.

"Did you give her the other one?" he asked Cis who had risen from her chair.

She shook her head to him and reached out her hand to take the kettle.

"Go for that parcel," he said to Marjie, and he sat on the arm of the settee.

"What's in it?" she asked him as she handed it to him.

"It's something for a very smart girl," he said and her father sounded proud. "You open it," he said and he left it with her.

She smelt what was in the brown paper before she could see it. And then she was ripping the paper, flinging it anywhere. It was a schoolbag, large, brown leather, with a pocket on the front. And it had straps to put over the shoulders. It was a day for Marjie's tongue to desert her.

"Well, what do you say? Will it do?" he asked, his eyes bright.

Marjie looked from the bag to her father's face. She was shy of what she read there and so she looked at the floor. "Ay," she said.

"That's my own present to you," he said. "For your books. So that they'll be right and you'll be like the rest. Now take that other thing you have and throw it."

"Where did Da get the money?" Marjie asked her mother after her father had gone back to the shed. Her father gave all his money for them.

"Your father was trying to keep a few pounds," her mother's hands were still holding her cup. "He wants to get an outboard engine for the boat. Finish your tea and go and look for that bairns for me. Tell them I've made tea."

The school bus picked the scholars up from The Corner. In the old days men pulled their boats up there, and later other men, wearing a different kind of uniform went away to fight for their country from there. It was where the three village streets met. Now, older men from the nearby houses would gather of a good evening to yarn and to impress the younger men with talks of their exploits and their big catches taken from wild seas.

Marjie stood with the others and waited. She knew these bigger boys and girls but she had never had much to do with any of them for not only did they live at opposite ends of the village but they seemed to be of a much more serious type altogether. So she kept her head down and looked at her new shoes. The older ones seemed sure of what they were doing. They laughed their hellos to the driver as they boarded the bus, and walked, without hesitation of any kind, to their seats. Marjie didn't know any driver so she slid past the man shyly and jumped into a seat somewhere about the centre of the bus and turned her eyes to the window. Her schoolbag felt large and awkward on her back and she couldn't sit straight. She felt strange and stiff in her new uniform. Her mother had washed her hair the previous night, and after Marjie had taken the basin up the stair for a proper wash, she sliced two inches from the bottom of it.

The journey seemed long. Marjie would have sat there and would never have got off, as she looked from the window to see the strange villages, farms and countryside going past. When a small girl with a mouse's face got on at one of the far away stops and asked through her nose, "Is that seat booked?" she wanted to say yes. She said no, however, and drew herself deeper into her blazer and went back to the window, seeing nothing for a time, feeling only the presence of the intruder beside her. When the small girl started coughing and sniffing she felt as though she would push her onto the floor. If she had to listen to sniffing she'd rather it was Jeannie's. Jeannie's sniffing was an extension of herself. After a time you didn't notice it. It was when she was quiet that you looked at her and wondered.

By the time the bus had rolled past the last stop and was speeding into the town and the Academy, nearly every seat was filled and it was very noisy. Loud laughter came from the big boys in the back seat and from some girls too. Many were new scholars like Marjie, easily identifiable by the newness of their uniforms and their shoes and their big schoolbags and the slightly lost look stamped on their faces.

When the bus pulled up outside the school gates there was a mad rush to the front. The big boys from the back elbowed through everybody and reached the door first. Marjie's schoolbag proved cumbersome and one of them wearing a crumpled shirt and a loose tie stood on her heel. When she bent to pull her shoe back on, in his hurry he sent her and the bag flying into an emptied seat. The school looked huge with hundreds of black and gold blazers streaming through the tall black gates and in the big front door. The mouse faced girl waited for Marjie and told her to come on. They called prayers 'assembly' in the Academy and there were a lot of teachers there.

She took three helpings of pudding at dinner. By following the one in front she managed fine. They gave tickets for dinner money. Marjie hadn't money so her tickets were stamped 'Free'. Marjie didn't mind. The dinner tasted the same. She stood with her tray of mince pie and cutlery and was at a loss where to go until the mouse faced girl, who told Marjie that her name was Margaret, called to her from a table at the back, "Sit here, Marjie. I kept you a place."

After dinner they wandered up into the town. Marjie didn't want to leave her good schoolbag but Margaret told her that no-one took their schoolbags and that no-one would touch it if she left it with the rest. They looked into the windows of the big shops. They were filled with cups and cakes and curtains and books and ointments. They walked past a grand hotel. "Mam's the cook in there," Margaret said. "She said we can go and

see her on Thursday." Marjie stood impressed. Afraid
they would be late into their new school they hurried
past places and rushed back. Then they spent their time
sitting on the grass and talked about the first half of their
day.

The Latin teacher had a look of Dannac, except that
Dannac didn't have a moustache and he wore different
clothes. He joked with the class and touched his moustache. There were twelve taking Latin and Margaret was
one of them. After he'd handed out the Latin Grammar
and a grey exercise book to each he told them they could
go to the shelf and take a book to read for the rest of
the period. Marjie read about Hector the Trojan who
killed Achilles. Achilles' mother dipped him into the
River Styx when he was a baby so that he would be
immortal. That meant he would live forever. Only she
gripped him by his heel, so that bit of him wasn't
immortal. And when Achilles was fighting against Hector
the Trojan in a battle, Hector the Trojan killed Achilles
in the heel with an arrow. It was a good story. Marjie
would like to know more about the people who lived in
Rome and Greece long ago. There was a man in Balmore
whose name was Hector and one of the fisher's drove a
trojan van.

The French class was twice as large as the Latin class.
The French teacher spent a good deal of the time diving
in and out of a huge cupboard, looking for the right
books to give them and for a smoke. He was easy with
the class and some of the most forward pupils answered
him back and he let them.

The enormous gold framed picture of the Academy's
founder frightened Marjie. He hung in the English room
and he nearly covered the whole of the back wall. His

face was alright. It was the long black coat he wore and the high winged collar which threw strange images before her.

The English teacher was grim. Very tall and grim. She was a woman and she sprayed them when she spoke. Heavily shod, she had them working from the minute they walked into her classroom, throwing a spelling book and a jotter onto each desk and telling them they should have pencils, that there was no point in coming if they hadn't one.

Completing the circle, the bus went over the station bridge on the way home. The boys at the back leapt from their seats and touched the roof with their heads and their loud whoops. The driver stopped the bus and spoke to them. He told them any more of that kind of nonsense and they could walk the four miles home. Marjie and Margaret sat tight in their seat and kept silent in case they would be thrown off too. One of the big boys at the back followed Margaret at her stop and tried to get past her. He was her brother.

"Remember to keep my seat tomorrow," Margaret called from the door.

"Ay," Marjie said to her. "Remember your home-work," and her mouth was glad and smiling.

Marjie had walked into another world. As she headed home through her village she felt as if she was bathed in a special kind of light, she felt as if every eye should turn to her. Her bag was heavy with books and jotters and there wasn't one mark on her blazer.

"Marjie," her Granny hailed her from her door. "I'm wanting you to get this cream for me tomorrow," she said. "I have it written for you," and she handed Marjie a piece of blue envelope and a two shilling bit. "And that's for yourself," and she pressed a sixpence into her hand.

Marjie wanted the sixpence. But she remembered her father's words. "Don't be taking money from your Granny. She hasn't it to give." And so her words of protest were weak. "Keep your money, Granny. I'll go for your cream for you. No bother." And when her Granny said, "Take it maital. That's for you," she breathed easy and put the sixpence into her pocket.

Arthur Morrison was on the road ahead of her. He was the only Hilltown pupil on the road and was late making home. The scholars arrived back in the village twenty minutes after the Hilltown ones.

Marjie didn't want to see his big goggly eyes or his big face or his big legs. And so she cut up Poor Benny's vennel for the back way home.

Peg was talking to her other neighbour on the other neighbour's step. They turned towards Marjie and smiled to her, then they went back to their speaking.

"How did you get on?" There was no-one in the house except her mother. She was sitting in her chair.

"Fine," Marjie said. "Where's everyone?" and she shrugged her bag onto the settee.

"Not far," her mother said. "Let me see that blazer."

"There's not one spot on it," Marjie stood before her. "You can look."

"What's that there?" her mother picked some imaginary thing from a lapel.

"There's nothing there," Marjie said. "Is there anything in it? I'm starving. You don't get tea with your dinner."

"Take yourself a piece of bread," her mother said. "What did you have?"

"We had mince pie and tatties. There was lumps in them. I nearly spewed. And steam pudding and custard. The custard was awful watery but I took thirds."

"And you tell me you're starving," her mother sighed. Her legs were spread before her, heavy and tired.

"They give you tickets for your dinner. Look," her tongue ran on between mouthfuls as she took the blue tickets from her inside pocket. "Look," she put them before her mother's face. "Free. See."

"Put them away," her mother said. "And when you've eaten that you can take that clothes off. I know you. Swanking about."

"Can I not keep anything on?"

"No, you can't keep anything on. What do you think I am? Washings?"

"Och."

"Never mind your och."

Up the stair in her old clothes Marjie didn't feel new any more. Her Red Cross skirt was baggy and scratchy and it hung below her knees. She thought of holding on to the shoes but her mother would be on her in a second and she didn't want to feel the weight of her mother's hand or whatever she had to hand that day.

"Can I go now?" she clattered down the stair.

"For five minutes," her mother said, and she was back to her looking at the dresser.

T W E L V E

Saturday night was wearing on. John Clark sat in his chair and re-checked his coupon.

"No," he said, his mouth full of disgust. "Nothing," and he screwed the piece of paper into a ball and tossed it into the fire.

"Are you going for a pint?" Cis asked from the other chair. "They'll be closing if you don't shift yourself."

"No, I'm not going for a pint. I'm feeling very weary," and his face was hanging on him.

"Good God man, a pint's not going to kill you. Get yourself off."

"No, I won't," he said.

"I hope you're not going to sit there all night with that face," she said.

"It's not my face that's wrong," he said and he rose from his chair and lifted the dry kindlers from the fender and put them into the box on the fender's end. "All I want is a little peace," he said from his crouched position.

"Peace!" she scoffed.

"Just let things be, will you," he pleaded with her. "I feel bad."

"You feel bad," she said. "You feel bad. What do you think I feel," her voice was rising.

"I know how you feel," he said back in his chair.

"You know! You know nothing," she was losing her control.

"If that's what you say," he said. His hands were spread on his knees and his head was bent to the floor.

"I suppose you think that you're the only one that's feeling bad. I don't suppose it would occur to you to think of anyone else."

"No, I don't think that," he said.

"Always in that shed," she kept on.

"Leave it, will you. The bairns'll hear," he said, and they both looked to little Paul in their bed, still sleeping.

"They're at it again," Marjie spoke from the blankets of her bed.

"They're always at it," Duncan said, wishing he could hide from the anger in his mother's voice.

"I hate it," said Marjie, and she put her head beneath the blankets.

"I hate it too," Jeannie said.

"I'm frightened," little Dan said, and he shook beneath the blankets with Duncan.

"I won't be long," he told her as he tightened the belt of his coat.

"Take all the time you want," she said and she took a ten shilling note from her purse and handed it to him.

"I don't want all that," he said. "Haven't you a half crown?"

"Take it," she said.

"Have you nothing less?"

"I have nothing less," she said.

He took it but he knew that the house needed the money more than he did. But there'd be no peace with her.

"I won't be long," he said and he stooped as he went through the door.

"Thank the Lord," Cis thought when she heard the outside door closing. He needed peace. Her laugh mocked her. Who didn't? Five minutes. That's all. Just give her five minutes without one of them wanting a part of her. All she ever heard was Ma this, and Ma that and Ma the next thing. Who was she? And when had she got a foothold inside her? When did she push Cissie Feeney out? And where was Cissie Feeney now?

She began to hum to herself. 'Veelia, oh Veelia.....' Cissie Feeney dressed like a lady and went to the opera. Her hair was the colour of the corn and many men wanted her. Cissie Feeney lived and died a long time ago. But she didn't know her. She only knew what came to live in her place.

She pushed the kettle onto the flames and reached her hand down the side of her chair for the catalogue. She began turning the pages, seeing nothing that was in it.

She had such hopes. Such hopes for them all. For John, for herself and for all of her bairns. But who could fight what they had before them? Even giving every ounce of what was in you, poverty would still grind you down.

She turned another page filled with clocks. She tried to steel her mind against the picture which kept intruding and which threatened to engulf her. That of Colin racing about on that motor bike. And Grace perched on the back as he took her to her friend in Balmore. That motor bike was the last thing that she needed. Her mind seemed to be crammed with worries. There didn't seem to be a place for anything else.

She made her tea quietly. The lot up the stair had ears like Radar and would pick up the sound of a teaspoon stirring. She put the cup to her lips and turned another page. That was a nice clock. She'd like a clock.

"Is he in yet?" were John Clark's first words when he came home.

"No," Cis said, her tone flat. There was a time when her mind couldn't worry any more. When she was all worried out. Then the mind just seemed to die or go to sleep or some other thing.

He had been true to his word, he hadn't been long. Half the time he'd been gone was spent in going and coming from the pub which was a mile from his house. His question was stupid. He knew that. The first thing he looked for when he came near to the house was the bike. It was nowhere. But when it was your own you always had to ask. In case. He walked from the room to the foot of the stair. "Come down," he called and they came like a bullet. They had been waiting, and listening. "There's packets of crisps here," he said and he pulled the cellophane packets from the inside pocket of his coat. They would have taken his hand from his wrist in their hurry.

Duncan was first there, taking the blankets halfway across the floor with him and leaving little Dan curled and quickly cold. For once Jeannie was quicker than Marjie. His voice interrupted Marjie's imaginings about the tall white columns of Ancient Greece and the Oracle at Delphi. One day she was going there. And she'd put her feet into the blue Aegean Sea. She wondered then if that sea was bluer than her sea. Herself and Margaret were going after they graduated from University. That would be in four years and there was plenty to learn in that time.

"Back up now," he said. "Keep warm. And mind your prayers." And they felt the safer for him saying the same words.

Any stranger walking into the room up the stair would have been forgiven for thinking they had walked into the middle of a quarry and were listening to the huge lumps of stone being turned into gravel. The only sound came from their jaws.

Marjie was the first one to finish, licking the salt from her empty bag. "She'll be making tea," she said and she put her tongue around her salty mouth. "Will we bawl for some?"

"You'll get hell if you do," Duncan said. "You'll get murdered," and he finished little Dan's crisps for him. When little Dan opened his mouth wide to yell, Duncan clamped his hand tightly over it. "You weren't wanting them," he told little Dan.

———————————

"I was talking to Jock Peg over," John Clark held his mug in one hand and his cigarette in the other.

"Did you have much. I bet you had a skinful," Cis said to him.

"What skinful? What are you talking about woman? I had nothing. One pint, that's all I had." He wished he hadn't. His guts was killing him. "I have your change," and he clapped his pocket.

"What did he want?" Cis asked. "I don't want change."

"Want? He didn't want anything. He told me Babsie's house is going."

"Who told him?"

"Lord, lassie, are they not the same family? Wasn't Babsie's man a cousin to Jock Peg?"

"How should I know?" she voiced her disinterest. "Everyone is related to everybody else up here."

"Anyway, it's going."

Cis said nothing. Her head was on her chest. She was following her own line.

"He said we should try for it," John Clark said after a time. "He seems to think that we might get it," and he threw the dregs from his mug onto the spent fire.

"What with? Sweets?" she kept her head bent.

Ay, what with? Himself had looked stupid at Jock Peg when he spoke to him in the bar.

"Just what you're needing, John," Jock Peg had said. "Now that the bairns are growing."

And he had told Jock Peg, he was straight with him. "I'll not deny that man," he said, "but I haven't a tosser. Now that's the truth to you," and they sipped their pints.

"Take a mortgage man," Jock Peg said.

"I don't know," he said. He had never thought of it. But he thought of the bairns up the stair. Big lassies and boys shouldn't be together like that.

"What do you think you could manage, John?" Jock Peg asked.

"Little," he had said to him.

"Well, if you're keen John, I'll tell you what I'll do," Jock Peg spoke fast. Sometimes all you could do was to watch his mouth.

"Oh, I'm keen enough," John Clark told him.

"Leave it to me John," Jock Peg said and he tapped the side of his nose with his forefinger. "MacLean of the Building Society is in the Mason's like myself. I'll speak to him on Wednesday night," and they drank the rest of their glass in silence.

He said to her, "Jock Peg's going to put a word in for me with MacLean at the Building Society. They're Masons," and he waited for her reply.

"You fool," she said. "We can't afford to pay up a house."

"We'll see," he said. "We have to try," and he showed her his empty hands.

The following Saturday John Clark met Jock Peg at the harbour.

"He's wanting you to go in," Jock Peg said as he came up the harbour steps from his boat.

"What did he say?" John Clark stood bowed beneath the weight of the outboard engine on his right shoulder.

"I told him what you said John, and he's wanting to see you. I would go quick if I was you. There's more that's after it," and he stood before him, nothing in his hands.

"I don't know what to be saying to you, Jock man. I'm grateful."

"Say nothing John. You're in work, you're making a wage. Go in as fast as you can. You'll not get him before Monday. He's there all day," and he nodded his glistening ball head to him. "If you don't get it John, I know the devil that will." He looked to the creels piled high in the stern of *The Girl Grace*. "You're putting some out," he said.

"Ach, one or two you know. I'm no getting them though. I only had two the last time. It'll not pay the petrol."

"No, nor petrol. They're not in it John. I don't know where they are but they're not in it," and Jock Peg walked up the harbour away from his boat. John Clark walked down the harbour to his.

Cis dragged her eyes from the clock as Colin came through the door. "What's it like out there now?" she asked him.

He shook his head to her. "You can't see your hand in front of you," he said. "And it's pitch dark."

"That didn't stop you going on that bike," she said. "Worrying people."

"No-one's asking you to worry," he was short with his mother. "Is there any sign of him?"

"No," she said. "He's been gone too long."

"I went over to the harbour. The boat's not back. I thought that he might have come into the bay. He'll likely make for the bay," and he came and sat in his father's chair.

The fog came out of nowhere and covered the coast and cut visibility to yards.

"Did you see anyone?" his mother asked Colin. "Did anyone see him on the sea?"

"I was speaking to Jock Peg but he only saw him when he was going out. Are you making tea?"

She swung the kettle onto the heat. "Turn that off," she said to Duncan at the wireless. Her voice was ragged with her anxiety.

"I'm only trying to get Radio Luxemburg," he turned the knob backwards and forwards.

"Never mind your Radio Luxemburg. Turn it off."

"Turn the thing off," Colin told him.

Marjie and Jeannie sat on the settee, white with what they saw written across their mother's face. Their Da would come soon. Their Da always came.

"He'll come," Colin said again, his brusque tone masking his concern as he took the cup from his mother.

"The rest of you can have this tea," she said and she made it for them. Her eyes were back on the clock. It must have stopped.

"When you've had that I want you to go to the shore with the torch," she said to Colin and Duncan and she jumped up and began raking in the bottom of the dresser.

"There's no battery in it," Duncan said, as she found out as soon as she lifted it.

She crouched before the open dresser door, beaten. Then she said, "The lamp. You can take the lamp," and she rose and lifted the lamp with the blue tin base from the top of the dresser. She shook it. "There's paraffin in it," she said. "There'll be enough. Finish that and take it," she urged them. She found the matches on the mantelpiece. "Take these," she said to Colin. "Take the lamp, Duncan. And mind you don't drop it. And put your jackets on," and she took them from the closet for them.

Outside it was like walking through cotton wool and never coming out of it. The light from their house and the other houses in the street peered through the fog like fading eyes. They felt their way to the gate by their hands and with their feet.

"Have you got that lamp, boy?" Colin's voice floated from somewhere backwards to Duncan.

"The lamp's fine," Duncan called back to the form somewhere on the road in front.

Their aim was to make for Beel's vennel which would take them straight to the shore. They thought they were following that line when a howl rang out from Colin.

"What's wrong with you?" Duncan sent his words into the mist. "Where are you anyway?"

"Over here," Colin called back. "Over here man. Where are you? I walked into a bloody dyke."

At last Duncan found Colin. He was bent over Mary Jean's back garden wall. "You're not anywhere near the vennel," Duncan told him.

"I know that," Colin's breathing came heavy. "I nearly broke my bloody knee."

"You nearly broke the wifie's dyke," he could hear the amusement in Duncan's voice. If it wasn't for the fog he'd wipe the grin from his laughing gob.

"Have you got that lamp, boy?" he growled. "Watch that lamp."

"The vennel's this way," Duncan said and he led, the lamp cradled into his chest as tenderly as any newly born baby.

They would have told anybody who cared to listen that they could find their way to the shore even if they were blind. The reality proved them wrong however. A yard too much this way and they were trying to climb someone's palings, a step too much that way and they were leaping from a grassy bank that had certainly moved since the last time they were there.

"Are you watching that lamp?" Colin roared to Duncan as he heard his distress call when his ankles buckled beneath him on the stony shore.

"Yes I have the lamp. There's nothing wrong with the lamp. It's me. I nearly broke my ankle."

"Cut the carry-on man," Colin's voice bore him no sympathy.

"Who's carrying on?" Duncan threw his voice to wherever it would land. "There's big stones on this shore."

Down at the small bay they stood together and spoke to one another.

"What now?" Duncan said, the lamp held before him the way the elder held the bible. Near to them, yet separated from them, was the sound of the sea as it broke over the rocks. In the greyness of that rocky shore they alone were existence. Colin now eighteen and Duncan, fourteen, two young men whose lives had always been bound up with the sea and who now refused to consider if it was their father that that sea would take this night.

"Are you hearing anything?" Colin peered for his boots.

"Nothing," Duncan said and he gouged a ditch into the sand with his heel.

They walked the length of the bay too many times to count, their paths crossing, not speaking. Their thought then was their own and they kept it to themselves. Duncan found the lamp an encumbrance yet he didn't know what he could do with it. Once they stopped and faced each other. "Did you hear that?" Duncan's voice was torn.

"What," Colin said, looking at the beads of moisture on Duncan's head.

"That. That there. Listen boy," and they put their heads to the side and tried hard to hear.

"I can't hear anything," Colin said.

"Ay," Duncan shook the hope from him. "It was nothing. It must have been something else," and he felt he would smash the lamp to smithereens right there on the shore. And they continued their walking.

"I'm soaking," Colin said. "Right through."

"Me too," Duncan said, and then his head went up, his voice filled with his jubilation. "By God, that's him. I was right. I was right," and if he cried in the fog in the dark, who was there to know or to see him.

"Give me the lamp," Colin said. "You take the matches," and his hand wouldn't find its way into his pocket. He could hear, as if it was coming from far off, the faint sound of an oar slapping the water. "Light the thing," he said to Duncan and he had the glass in his other hand.

The first match died on them. They huddled more closely around the second one and cupped their hands about it. It too spluttered and died in the darkness. "Will you light the bloody thing?" Colin's voice was wretched. "He'll be on the bloody rocks." The third match flared and they put it to the wick. The wick burned. "Get the glass on. Quick," Colin's hands would do nothing for him. "Turn it up a wee bit," Duncan said, and he took the drip from his nose with the back of his hand. "Not that high," he cried when the flame leapt through the top of the glass. "Ay, that's it. That should do it," when Colin had got the flame right.

They stood with the lamp at the water's edge. "He's coming," Colin said, and there was a note almost of holiness in his voice. "He's on the oars," he said to cover what he might show.

Duncan had the lamp once more. He held it high like the Olympic flame. "He's taking an awful long time," he said.

"Give it to me," Colin took his turn and stood like a warrior.

"Sound travels clear over water. He's likely quite a long way out yet." He waved the lamp in an arc above his head, and kept on doing it, high and wide.

And then *The Girl Grace* parted the grey shrouds and came home, sweet and true and well clear of the rocks, their father a ghost man bent to his oars.

"Did your mother send you?" were the first words he spoke. They could see him clawing for his breath as he ran her aground.

"Ay," they said, the water about their legs as they pulled the boat up for him, their bodily strength saying what their tongues found it impossible to.

"I was just making for home," he took his time on the sand. "Down it came. A right pea-souper I can tell you."

"Did you get all the creels set?" Colin spoke to him of normal things.

"Oh, I got them set alright. I tell you no man should be out there this night. I kept looking for Wood's light," they could hear the rattle from his chest. "I was lost," and he shook his head. He took the outboard from the stern and began to hitch it up on to his shoulder.

"I'll take that," Colin said, and he led the way. He had his father's height and he walked strong and straight for him. His father walked behind him and Duncan followed with the lamp.

"I'll just stop here," their father said as they tackled the bank, and they stood with him. He bent himself and they looked to his shoulders heaving from the effort he had had.

"Are you alright?" Colin asked him.

"Keep going," John Clark's voice was strong, and Duncan released his breath.

Their mother chased them to bed early that night. Arguments about going to bed at half past nine like a bairn she wouldn't listen to. She wanted them out of her sight and that's all there was to it. Colin was quite happy to go. He took the wireless and Radio Luxemburg to the closet. Little Paul could go to his bed anytime. He just climbed up into the big bed.

"I was speaking to Jock Peg over at the harbour," John Clark said. His mug was in his hand and his bonnet was steaming on the fender. Three jackets were draped over chairs. The room smelt of warm damp wool intermingled with the faint smell of singeing.

"You're burning that hat," Cis said as she turned the jackets and he moved it away from the direct heat.

"I'm going in to see MacLean," he said. "In fact I think I'll phone him first."

"Well, you'll have to phone, won't you," she turned a sleeve's inside to the fire. "Or I could drop him a line for you."

"That would do," he said and he reached to the grate for the teapot and poured tea into his mug.

"If it caught the first post on Monday, he'd have it on Tuesday," she told him, her hand patting jackets for dry places. She rose from her chair and pushed it against the wall, away from the fire. Then she brought the wooden chairs and their clothes tight in against the fender. "If you give me these trousers," she said, "I'll dry them for the morning. Then I'm going to bed."

"Ach, they're not bad," he said and he ran his hands up and down his thighs, felt the bottoms of them.

She bent before him and felt the corduroy he was wearing.

"They're wringing, man," she said.

––––––––––––––––

"Is Da going on my bus? People don't go on school buses," Marjie said that morning. There was a large streak of soot on the collar of her white blouse. She had never learned to wipe the iron when she took it from the fire.

"I'm going on the first bus," John Clark was trying to

shave in the middle of them. He had to take the day off from his work and he didn't want to waste it.

"You'll be too early. The man won't be there till nine," Cis spread their bread for them.

"The morning he said. I'll wait," John Clark said. "I want to get this out of the way. The quicker I'm there, the quicker I'll be out," he drew the razor down his cheek. "I'm going out to the sea in the afternoon if all's well. No use in wasting the whole day."

"Oh get out of my way the lot of you," Grace was trying to hold her place in front of the big mirror. She was teasing her hair into a style and was afraid to lay the comb down in case someone snatched it. She held it between her teeth.

"I told you about that iron," her mother said to Marjie. "The collar of that blouse is filthy."

Marjie lifted her head to her mother with an uncomprehending look, then she dived back into the interior of her schoolbag.

"Who took my geometry jotter?" she asked.

"Nobody touched anything," her mother said.

"Well, someone must've, because it's not here," she accused everyone.

"Who'd be wanting your geometry jotter?" Duncan asked as he ducked and weaved behind Grace in his effort to see a corner of the mirror.

"Well, someone did," Marjie was beginning to fret after her second fruitless search.

"You heard what I said," her mother said. "There was no-one near your bag," and she was rough on little Dan's face with the flannel.

"I saw Ma taking pages out of it to write on," Jeannie's piece was halfway up her face.

"You little witch," her mother pushed little Dan from her. "Did anyone see me touch that book?" she appealed to them.

"No," Duncan was trying to do things to his hair with Colin's Brylcream.

John Clark kept quiet and out of it.

"She put it under the cushion of the chair," Jeannie said.

"Oh, my jotter," Marjie bounded to her mother's chair and lifted the cushion. Feverishly she opened it and turned the pages. "Half of it's torn out," she bawled and waved the blue jotter to anyone who would look. "I'll get it from the teacher."

"Shut your face," her mother warned, "or I'll give you something to cry about."

"Well, I'm not going to school," Marjie said to her, and she threw herself onto the settee, her face a crumpled mess.

"You'll get yourself out that door, my girl," her mother was over to her in two strides. "I'll give you a jotter," and her hand was very heavy.

Marjie's howl was horrible.

"I'm getting out of this place," Grace said and she grabbed her handbag and walked away from them, throwing the comb to Duncan.

"What a house this is," John Clark said and he stuck a piece of cigarette paper onto the nick on his chin. "It's a wonder my whole face is not off."

Jeannie was quiet. She'd done enough.

Duncan had the comb and the mirror to himself. He was early with his grooming. He didn't need to leave the house for another half hour but there was no point in wasting opportunity. It might not come again for a long while.

He combed his dark hair forward on to his brow in its usual fashion. He stood and looked at what was looking back at him. He was tired of looking the same and so he raked the comb backwards making his hair stand up like a hedgehog's spikes. He rubbed another liberal amount of Colin's Brylcream between his palms and fiercely worked it through his hair. He looked at himself again. Then he thought of Colin's big fist when he found his jar was half empty and he flattened it again.

"Are you going to get out that door?" Cis had little Dan girning with the force of the hand which wielded the comb.

"No," Marjie's defiance was strong.

"I won't tell you twice," her mother said and she put little Dan from her and dragged Marjie from the settee.

"I'm not going like this," Marjie said. "People'll see me. Everyone'll know I was crying," and as her mother struggled against her young strength Marjie's left foot shot out and struck her mother on the shin.

"You bitch," her mother nearly took her head from her shoulders. "You wicked little bitch," and her mother crawled brokenly for her chair.

"Are you still going at it?" John Clark had come from the back with the empty basin in his hand.

"She kicked Ma," Jeannie was on no-one's side.

"I never did," Marjie's fear brought the lie to her lips. "She tripped on my feet."

Her mother was a heap in the chair.

"You," her father pointed his finger at Marjie. "Out that door. Wherever you are there's trouble. I don't know what this house is coming to. And the rest of you," he turned to the quiet ones. "Get your grub and then get yourselves up that brae to school so that your mother can have a little peace."

"What am I going to say to the teacher?" Marjie's defiance was subdued. "She even tore out my triangles. They were my homework. I'll be in for trouble," and she put the jotter into her bag and buckled it.

"Who's she?" her mother was ready for more. "The cat's mother."

"It's you that'll be in for trouble," Marjie's defiance returned at the door. "You'll likely have the rector down at you," and she left her battlefield behind her. She could still hear her mother's voice shouting things when she reached Beulah's.

She was at the shop before she realised her father was on the road not far behind her. Well, he needn't think she was going to slow down for him. Any other day she would have. Her belly was sore on Saturday night when he was never coming home from the sea. It was even sore all through doing her geometry homework but she never told anyone. And when herself and Jeannie went to the well in the fog it was as sore as anything then and she could hardly carry the pail. She didn't want to walk on the road with him, didn't want even to see him, to see his eyes. It was right, she acknowledged to herself as she walked to catch the school bus that morning, there did always seem to be trouble wherever she was. Or wherever she or any of her family was. She was never in trouble away from the house. She always seemed to be in trouble with her mother. She knew that. But she didn't think that she was the sole cause of it. But she was always getting it. Was that because she was always doing it? It must be, she thought and she drove a stone from the centre of the road with the toe of her shoe.

She turned her head very slowly so that he wouldn't know, and looked over her shoulder. She saw that he was getting nearer and so she quickened her steps.

At the corner she stood apart from the other scholars and looked at her feet. When he reached her, he came to stand beside her.

"Tell your teacher that it was the baby that did it," he said. "And if there's any trouble, tell me," and there was concern on him as he looked on the downbent head. "She'll surely understand about your triangle things."

"He's a man teacher," she said and still she wouldn't look at him. "I was going to say about the baby anyway," and she lifted her head and tried to stand easy with him. He looked like a different Da in his suit, taller, straighter. He only wore his good bonnet when he went to the pub or the church. Her Da normally smelt of the sea and lug and his cigarette smoke, smells that you never knew were there until they weren't anymore.

"That's me off then," he said as the passenger bus passed along the top road before it descended the brae to them. "Are you wanting a threepenny?" and he stretched his closed hand to her. And then he said what he always said when one of them was leaving him. "See and watch yourself now."

He let Grace and the other working girls go in front of him. She saw him speaking to the girls and they laughed with him. "A return," she heard him say to the conductress and he made a joke with her as he handed her his money and they both laughed. Then he had a word with the driver sitting in front of him. It was a long time since she had seen her Da this way, laughing and joking with people. At times she forgot that things had ever been like that.

Grace and the girls settled themselves near the back. At the corner they formed a separate scented huddle and talked of grown up things. Coats and handbags didn't mix with blazers.

As the bus pulled away from them and they waited for their own to come Marjie felt like that bairn again. She wanted to cry because her father was going away from her.

———————————

"We're getting a new house," Jeannie was on the dyke waiting for Marjie to come home. She was full of her news. "I'm going to be dressed every day in our new house."

"What?" Marjie's bag was at her heels.

"You can ask Ma," Jeannie was a ballet dancer now with the palings her barre.

"Oh stop your jumping will you. When are you going to grow up?" Marjie wasn't in the mood for Jeannie and her uncomplicated ways.

"I told you," the Sugar Plum Fairy said. "Ask Ma. She'll tell you," and she pranced after Marjie up the path.

"Is it true what she said?" Marjie burst in on her mother. "Are we getting the house?"

"You heard," her mother said from her chair.

"See," Jeannie pirouetted near the table.

"When?" she asked.

"When things are seen to," her mother said.

"You don't sound very pleased about it then," Marjie said and she sat on the arm of the other big chair.

Her mother sighed.

"How? What's wrong?" Marjie asked.

"I don't want to go over there," her mother said.

"It's nearer the school," Jeannie said and she lifted a handful of sugar from the bowl.

Her mother looked at what Jeannie was at but for once she said nothing.

"Why don't you want to go over there?" Marjie tried again.

Her mother shook her head. "You wouldn't understand," she said.

"Is Da out in the boat?" she asked her mother.

"Ay," Jeannie said.

"Have we got much money?" Marjie asked her mother.

"No, we haven't got much money," her mother mimicked Marjie. "As a matter of fact, we've no money," and with a vicious jab she drove the poker into the fire.

"How are you going like that?" Marjie asked. "Are you not wanting another house?"

"Don't talk soft girl," she gave her mirthless laugh again. "You don't know what you're talking about," and the wood on the fire got it again.

THIRTEEN

It was October again when they left the half-house. Colin drove the tractor and trailer and Duncan stood stooped on the back, holding fast to its mudguards. The new house wasn't far from their old house, and so it was easier for them this time.

They were going to a solid stone house, warm and dry with three bedrooms and a kitchen with a tap. Still there was no inside toilet, but there was a lavatory, which flushed, at the back. The tap cut out the trips to the well, and the lavatory cut out the trips to the shore with the slop pails.

They managed to gather some decent pieces of furniture to fill this larger house. One day John Clark came home with a television set for them and the little ones acquired a small grey cat from the farm above them.

Marjie created the most noise at their leaving for nowhere could she lay her hands on the new black trousers her mother took from the catalogue for her. She hunted up the stair and down, high and low and everywhere, but they were nowhere, not even a shade of them was to be seen.

"He must've taken them," she told her mother when Colin was leaving the house.

"I never touched your trousers. What would I be wanting them for?" Colin flared from the doorway.

"Well, you must have. They're nowhere."

"I never touched them. Right." and he came back into the room to punch her on the arm.

That didn't shut Marjie's mouth. She'd had worse from him. "You did so, you big brat," she said. "I bet you took them to clean your car."

"Will you be quiet?" her mother was at her back. "If he says he didn't see them, he didn't see them. You'd make trouble in an empty house, you would."

John Clark lifted the two little ones up into the trailer, among the chairs and the beds, then he swung himself up beside them.

"You can go now," he called to Colin. "Easy now," and he put an arm about each of them.

Only Grace was missing from among them. "I'm away up to Anne's," she announced as soon as she came from her bed, not a drink of tea inside her. "I'm not staying here for people to see us flitting with a tractor," and she clenched her teeth and her head shook. "Oh, I can't stand it. I'll be home the night."

"Is there anybody out there?" her mother asked Marjie as she stood in front of the bare window.

"Only Peg and Mrs MacIntyre standing at Peg's gate."

"I want to get out before anybody sees me. Always looking," her mother said and she buttoned her coat up to her chin.

"They'll only be wanting to say cheerio to you," Marjie

was impatient to be off.

"Come on then," her mother said and called to Jeannie from the stair she was sitting on.

"And close that door," she instructed Marjie as they walked from their house for the last time.

The day was bright and clear with that sharpness to it which comes at that time of the year.

"Give me your hand," her mother said to Jeannie and they walked down the path and through the gate to Peg and Mrs MacIntyre.

"That's it then Cis," Mrs MacIntyre nodded, one hand in her apron pocket. Her eyes were sad. "See you'll not forget us now."

"We'll miss you, and the bairns," Peg said and she blinked behind her glasses. "You'll look over to see us sometime."

"Yes, yes I will," Cis was already moving away. "Chee-rio," she had no other words. She tugged at Jeannie's hand to stop her prancing. "Keep still, will you. Who do you think you are, Margot Fonteyn?"

"Are you glad you're going to your new house Ma?" Jeannie asked when she was still.

"Ay, ay I'm glad hinny," and her grip on Jeannie's hand tightened.

They walked past many people on the road that morning. Some were going and many were coming back. It was Saturday morning and the whole place was about.

Beulah was coming from the shop. "You're going into your new house today," she said to them. "I heard," and her twinkling eyes were young. "Benny forgot the semolina," she explained to them and she showed them the packet. Then she reached out her other hand and touched their mother's arm. "God bless, lassie," she said and walked on.

"She called you lassie," Marjie said before Beulah was clear of them.

"Be quiet, you," her mother didn't look pleased. "That woman'll hear you."

"Come and see the tap, Ma," little Dan tugged his mother through the door, past the boxes and upturned furniture. "This is the kitchen," he told her. "Look," and he turned the tap as hard as he could. "Real water," he said and the real water washed the window, the walls, himself and his mother with its force.

"Turn it off, turn it off," his mother said to him as his wrist struggled to undo what he'd done. No more well, she thought. Thank the Lord for that. "Where's the kettle?" she asked little Dan, who had managed to stop the flood. "Find me the kettle," and they walked into the living room.

"Which beds do you want where?" John Clark called down from the stair landing.

"We're taking this room," Marjie told her father as she and Jeannie stood in its doorway to guard it against anyone else.

"Our bed's going in here," she said.

"They can have that one," Jeannie told him, looking to the room across from them.

"Where's the bairns?" Cis had filled the kettle and was looking for little Paul.

"He's here with me," Duncan called from the down bedroom at the other end of the house.

"There's a bathroom up the back," little Dan couldn't keep his legs still with the excitement that was in him. "It's in a wee shed. You just have to pull a handle down and you get water."

"It's a lavatory," Jeannie swanned down the stair to tell him. "Are you coming to see it?" she asked the ignorant one.

"And someone's left coal and a pan in the shed," he told his mother at the top of his voice.

"Keep out of that filth, you," his mother caught his shoulder and dragged him to a chair. "Sit there," she said.

"Is there any tea in it?" John Clark's voice sailed down the stair again.

"Has anyone seen the teapot?" Cis was looking into boxes.

"It's in this one," little Dan left his chair to be helpful. "Here, Ma," and he put it into her hand.

"Now, find me the other things and I'll make you all a cup of tea," his mother said to him.

"Now," John Clark told them when they were taking their tea. "This is our house, our own house, but it'll have to be paid for." They looked at him and waited for him to carry on.

"If we all do our best we should manage," and he looked around them all. Colin was with them, he had gone back over for his car. Colin was taking in a good wage, keeping them sometimes. Grace wasn't taking in so very much, shops paid nothing and what with her fares. She was only a lassie and she liked clothes and the dancing. Duncan would finish at the school in the summer. Duncan was clever and could do something. Maybe train for a mechanic or whatever. He could ask at one of the garages for him when the time came. Of course apprentices were paid nothing and had to take their tools from it, but still and all. Marjie was the next one. It would be a while before she was finished with the school. And what then? She was bright. Too bright sometimes. Her mother's people were like that, quick. And then there was the three littler ones. Their time would come too. He was in work just now, and he could always fall back on the ditching if the worst came. He could do that.

"That's it then," he said and he rose. "You come up the stair with me," he said to Duncan. "I'll need you to give me a hand with this beds," and he took his mug to the sink.

"When are you going to put the aeriel up for the T.V.?" Duncan asked, but he went with him.

"Whenever I'm ready," his father would have no argument.

"I was wanting to watch 'Laramie'. Everyone's speaking about it. Everyone gets to see it," he followed his father to the top of the stair.

"Everyone, is it?" his father said. "Now, I want you to catch that end of this bed and hold it until I tighten the nuts."

John Clark sat in his chair by the fire, little Paul wedged into the corner beside him. Across from him Duncan sulked in the other armchair. Drying clothes blocked the fire from Marjie and Jeannie and little Dan on the sofa. There was laughing and joking between them.

"It's like Auschwitz in here," Cis sat on a wooden chair beside the door and twisted her hands.

"What do you know of Auschwitz?" John Clark said. His tone was sharp with her as he crossed one leg over the other.

"Well, it's freezing," she said and she hung her head to the side.

"Sit here," he jumped up from his chair. "One of you," he spoke to them on the sofa, "move that jackets till your mother'll get a warming."

"I don't want to sit there," she said.

"Come in," he coaxed her. "Come in to the heat."

"I don't want to come in to the heat. I'm alright as I am," she said. She wrung her hands tighter then began to pull at her fingers. Jeannie and Marjie looked at each other and said nothing.

"You can sit in my place," Marjie said, but she still sat.

"I'm alright," their mother said.

Duncan came from his sulk. He knew that like this his mother wouldn't notice him sneaking through to switch the television on. In her right state she would brain him because that room was for keeping, not for big lazy ones to lie around watching T.V. in all night.

"Come on lass," his words to her were soft, and he held her hand. "You're alright now," and she looked at him and he knew that wherever she was he couldn't follow.

All that he could do was wait, wait for her to come out of it. He left her and went to the chair with the drying working clothes and he began to turn them to the heat. Colin had been to his waist in water at the ditches again.

He sat down in his chair. They'd all scattered ben but he hadn't the heart to chase them through. They were doing no harm. He looked across to her and shook his head. She'd be that way till she came from it. He reached into the coal pail for two lumps of coal and placed them on to the fire.

Marjie didn't run to the shore anymore when her mother took bad. She stood at the open window of the bedroom she shared with Grace and Jeannie and listened to the waves as they rumbled and broke on the rocks. When lying in her bed with Jeannie she could float away on that sound, clear through the window and away. The tattie holidays would be starting soon, on Friday. If she'd stayed in Hilltown School she'd have had three weeks in which to earn money. As an A pupil at the Academy she would only have the one week. Of course if she brought in a letter she would be granted the two weeks exemption that every pupil was legally entitled to, but being an A pupil she wasn't expected to ask for it. When she told her mother this her mother gave her a row. "You'll take three weeks. Get me my pad. I'll give them something to think of. One week! What good is one week to anyone?" Marjie handed the letter to the rector and he told her she could have the extra fortnight if she thought that it was absolutely essential and that she would have to work hard to make up for what she missed when she returned. Marjie told him that it was absolutely essential and thanked him, sir.

The sounds from the television drifted up to her. Her mother would murder them, she was trying to keep that room good. She moved back from the window and sat on Grace's bed. It'd be hers when Grace left. The sound of the waves reached her and she let herself go with them. Floating, floating away. But away where to? She didn't know. But she knew what she would float away from. Away from the fear that lived inside her, away from the poverty that stamped the outside of her. At fourteen she was aware of it as the young child she was, but had never been. Away from herself, this being who was different. She had always felt this difference, even among her brothers and sisters she had recognised its face. And there were times when she didn't like it, when she wanted to turn from it and never feel it again. And then she tried to live with sameness. But that only worked for a short time. Then different would come back at her and she didn't know what way to be. And so she put her head in the sand and dreamed herself out of what she had no power to change.

She heard the silence from the room directly beneath her. She wondered what way her mother was. Her schoolbag was down there, behind the armchair where she dropped it. She could be doing her homework. And she thought of Lars Porsenna of Clusium and the nine gods he swore by. If she crawled back down she'd get sworn at.

Her mother was herself again. "Keeping lazy buggers in school," she cried from the same chair as Marjie's hand gripped the bag's shoulder strap. "You can get this place tidied up. Get these dishes done."

"I'm coming, I'm coming," Marjie, still crouched behind the chair, her arms about her head as she fended the blows which she saw coming.

"I'll sort you out my girl," her mother had lifted the poker from the fire place and Marjie's raised elbow caught it.

"Can I not turn my back for five seconds?" John Clark had been to the coal shed for a shovel of dross for the back of the fire. "Come from there," he ordered, "before my clock'll get it. What's it all about this time?" and his words were weary.

"She hit me with the poker," Marjie sobbed to her father.

"Who's she? The cat's mother," her mother had laid the poker on the hearth.

"She nearly broke my funny bone," Marjie's voice was in bits. "My hand's sore," and she cradled her aching hand with the other one.

"I don't know. I just don't know," he said and as he bent to place the dross on top of the coals he was an old man. "This can't go on, you know," and he turned and looked from the fire to Cis.

"That's right, take her side. Where do you think you're going?" she cried at Marjie as she came from behind her chair. "You're not going near that T.V."

"I'm not," Marjie knuckled the tears from her eyes. "You said I've to wash the dishes," and she ducked her head beneath the low doorway.

The warm dishwater soothed the ache from her hand. She trailed it through the soap and felt the trap close.

"You'd best leave that," her father said as she was drying the plates. "Your mother's going out. Go with her for me."

"I'm going on my own. I don't want her," her mother's voice carried through to the kitchen.

"Where will you go?" he was stooped with care.

"I don't know," and she tied her headscarf below her chin.

"Keep to the street lights," he cautioned her. "It's a black night."

"You think I'm stupid. It's not a child you're talking to," she turned on him.

"Go with her," her father said to Marjie as her mother walked through the door.

Marjie hated the late night walks. Her heart was heavy with dread at every step she took. The walks had started some time ago, since her mother came to their new house. Grace used to go then. But Grace stayed with her friend some nights and then Marjie went.

"What way are you wanting to go?" she spoke to her mother as she hesitated where the road forked.

"How should I know?" her mother still sounded angry with her and Marjie wished that she was at home. "Away. Just away," her mother said.

Marjie walked closely at her mother's heels. The stars were out and the moon was riding high. Across the road and over the bank the sea moaned in the night.

"Don't walk behind me," her mother said to her. "You're catching my heels."

"Where are you going to?" Marjie asked as the street lamps shone over them.

"Well, if you must know, I'm going to see Jessie, that's all."

Now that her mother had a fixed destination Marjie's

mind was easier and her step was lighter. She knew Jessie. Jessie had lived in Balmore like they did, then moved back to Hilltown as soon as there was an empty house. They walked past the curtained windows.

"You needn't come any further," her mother said when they came in sight of Jessie's house, the lighted windows signalling that Jessie was at home. Marjie didn't know what to do. She stood and looked at her mother. "You heard," she said, her hand on Jessie's gate.

"Will someone come to meet you?" Marjie didn't want to leave her.

"Go home," her mother said and banged the gate behind her. "I don't want her seeing you."

Marjie watched her mother knock on Jessie's door and she heard the welcoming surprise in Jessie's voice when she opened it to her visitor. Her mother stepped into Jessie's house and the door was closed.

Marjie stood with her back to Jessie's hedge and let the darkness enfold her. The sound of a door slamming further along the street brought her back and she turned for home. The moon came from behind a cloud and she didn't feel so alone any more. '*And still they say of a winter's night, When the wind is in the trees, And the moon is a ghostly galleon, Tossed upon cloudy seas*'. Her mind crooned Alfred Noyes' words every time she looked on a night-time moon.

She caught the wind in a garden sycamore and she wished that she could follow. Passing the old schoolhouse she saw a ghost and her heart nearly knocked her teeth from her mouth, so great was its hurry to escape from her chest.

———————

"She said I had to go home," she told her father when she was back in the house. "I saw a ghost."

"I'll take a walk over to meet her in a couple of hours," he said. "Did she ask for anyone to come?"

"She just told me to go home," Marjie said. She sat on the arm of the settee. Her heart was still thumping with the ghost.

"Tell that ones to put that television off. I'm going to make them their tea."

"You've to get," Marjie spoke to Duncan. He and Jeannie and little Dan and little Paul stared with unblinking eyes at the images on the screen in front of them. No-one looked at Marjie and no-one spoke. Duncan had thrown himself across an armchair, his back was resting against one arm, his legs hung over the other.

"I said you've to get. All of you," Marjie's voice was louder this time.

Jeannie and little Dan and little Paul were perched on the edge of the settee. They gazed and breathed as one.

"Right," Marjie stamped over to the switch. "That's going off," and the room went silent when the sound from the corner died.

"Leave that alone. We're watching that," Duncan came from his chair like a stone from a catapult. "Put that back on," he growled and his balled fist caught Marjie beneath her left eye.

"Da said," she told him and her foot flew to his shin.

"I was watching that," he turned the switch to 'on' again.

The three on the settee kept breathing and out of it.

"Well, I'm just telling," she nearly took the door with her when she went out.

Her father was in the kitchen waiting for the kettle to boil. "Tell them I'm coming," he said and he put milk into five cups. "There's been nothing but trouble in the house ever since that thing came."

FOURTEEN

"That's the second week she's sent nothing," Cis cried after the postman had passed. "She's going to get a mouthful from me. Get me my pad," she said to little Dan.

Ever since joining the W.R.A.F. one year before with her friend Anne, Grace's letters had dropped onto the mat on every Wednesday morning. Now, it was Saturday for the second time, and still nothing.

"She's not going to get off with it. Thinks she's so high and mighty. Keeping every penny. Well, I'll show her. She can get herself home here."

"We can't mark anymore," Jeannie threw the message bag onto the settee. "He says when we pay what's owing we can get more."

"Give me that note," her mother's voice was climbing. Jeannie took the slip of paper from the bag and handed it to her.

"Take it to Nan's," there was pleading in her voice to Marjie. "Tell her she'll get paid next week."

"I'm not going," Marjie set her face against her mother. "I'm tired of asking."

"You'll take that messages note and you will go," her father's voice was hard to her before he went out.

"What's all the racket about now?" Colin came into the house, wiping the oil from his hands with someone's vest. "The whole place can hear you."

"Let them," his mother's voice was wild. "Let everyone hear."

Marjie and Jeannie looked across to one another with clamped mouths.

"Is there anything in it to eat?" Colin asked.

"No, there's nothing in it to eat. They won't give us anything," his mother told him.

"What are you doing with the money anyway?" his words attacked her.

"My best. My bloody best," she cried back at him. If he was shorter he would have felt the weight of her hand.

"You're getting plenty," he was merciless as he drove on.

"Did you hear that?" she looked to them all. "Getting plenty am I? Well, you get yours on your back," she flung at his face.

"Give me that note," Marjie could have torn it from her mother's hand. "I'll go to Nan's," and she was glad to be out of it. Cis sat awhile. "Tell your father I want him," she said to Jeannie, and Jeannie looked at her mother's face and went up to the shed.

"What is it now?" John Clark's breaths were becoming shorter. He hung in the doorway, one hand pressed against the upright of the door.

"Come in," Cis said. "I want to talk to you. There's been no money from that one again."

"Nothing eh?" he stooped to rest his hands on the back of the settee. "What's she playing at?" Beads of sweat stood on his brow.

"Well, I'll soon settle her. She can get herself home here."

"Is she due leave?"

"Never mind leave. I'm writing to the head man to tell him I'm ill and I can't manage without her."

"I don't think you should be doing that. You can't go interfering. Best to write to her how things are and can she send something."

"Interfering?" she shouted to him. "I'm her mother and she'll do what I want. She's coming home."

"Well, you know best," his speech was thin. "I'm going to the shed."

"Bloody shed," she muttered as he left. "Where's my pad?" she pounced on Jeannie. "She's not half going to get it."

Jeannie looked at her mother and said nothing. Grace was always getting it. Jeannie liked Grace coming home. She took presents to everyone of them. She took Colin polish for his car. The socks she was wearing came from Grace. They were luminous green and made her legs look nice.

"And you can leave that fire alone," her mother said to her when she would disturb the mound of caked dross with the poker. "Style, that's her trouble," she continued and the biro darted over the page. "I'll give her style. Who does she think she is?" She expected no answer from Jeannie nor did she get one. Jeannie's nose was buried in the pages of one of Grace's teenage magazines. She'd done something with the straight fringe which she'd worn for as long as she could remember. At thirteen she was becoming interested in hairstyles. Her fringe now hooked upwards and out: cups could hang from it.

"She can get herself work here," her mother railed on. "And help me with the home." Her mother spoke to the top of Jeannie's head. Jeannie's sniff was quiet so as not to irritate her mother further.

"You took your time," Colin threw a bucket of cold water over the bonnet of his car. He was wearing his good clothes. With the car between them Marjie gave him a look that told him plenty and none of it was good.

"Did she give you them?" her mother was taking the floorcloth across the tiles on the fireplace.

"She didn't have Capstans. I took Players," Marjie threw herself and the bagful onto the settee.

"What did she say?" her mother's voice was filled with her eagerness to know, as she checked the contents of the bag.

"She didn't say anything. I told her you said we would pay next week." Marjie's breath was quick on her. She'd walked as fast as she could go and the bag was heavy with the sugar and the loaves and the syrup.

"Was she alright?" her mother called from the kitchen as she stooped before the cupboard.

"Ay. She never said anything. She put two extra sweeties in the bag for myself." And I ate at least six, Marjie thought.

"You've been eating these sweets," her mother had the uncanny knack of seeing what was in her mind.

"I wasn't," Marjie called through to her. "I only ate the two she put in for me," she lied straight through her chocolate coated teeth.

"I wasn't born yesterday," her mother was easier for having the messages in her cupboard. "That bag's half empty."

"Well, it was half full when I last saw it," Marjie spluttered. There was no way of denying the evidence which her mother had thrust under her nose.

"Take these to your father," she said and she handed Marjie the packet of Players.

"Is she making anything?" Colin was on his back beneath his car.

"I don't know," Marjie growled to him and walked clear of his large blue suede feet.

"What did the post take?" John Clark tapped the end of his cigarette on its packet.

"Nothing," Cis said.

"What took him to the house then?"

"We got a coupon from Oxydol," Jeannie was enjoying her bacon roll.

"Oh, that was all," he lifted his mug to his mouth.

"That was all," Cis said, and her look bored through Jeannie.

She thought of the brown envelope which she carried in her apron pocket. She carried its contents deeper than that. She didn't need to open it to know. It would say the same as the other two which ended up in the back of the fire.

"I wrote to her," she said to him.

"Put it in the fire," he said. He shook his head. She'd spoil things with them yet.

"I won't put it in the fire," she tore a piece from her roll and put it into her mouth. "Anyway, it's away. Jeannie put it in the post."

"There's no need for all this, you know," he had no other words with her. "Making trouble."

"There'll be no trouble. You'll see. She just needs to be shown who's boss," and she lifted her cup.

The thud of Grace's kitbag as it landed on the lobby floor told them she was home. They paused with their forks in the air. She came into the room like thunder. Her heart had stopped in its beating when the yellow envelope was handed to her. No breath was in her. "Do you want me to open it for you?" the girl from Reading asked her. The girl from Reading was nice. She managed to shake her head as she made a neat corner with the sheet. With her useless hands she tore at the envelope. "Come home at once," the words on the Post Office form read. "Mother ill." Six words. And she knew that they were going to change her life. She would always get her, no matter where she went.

"I thought you were sick," she couldn't say that other word.

"I am," her mother was making the tea. "I'm very sick."

"Rita from next door was on the bus. She was surprised to see me home again so soon. I told her you were very sick and that I got a telegram. She said it was a wonder that she hadn't heard," and she tore her hat from her head and placed it on the dresser. Her long dark hair was pinned clear of her collar and she wore golden hoops in her ears.

"Nosey parker," her mother dismissed her neighbour.

"I felt such a fool," Grace's eyes flooded with what she had kept to herself for too long.

"Sit down here," her father's voice was gentle for her. "Did you have anything to eat?"

"I can't eat," she said, taking his chair.

"Drink that," he said and he pressed the cup of tea into her hands.

"What are you all looking at?" Grace glared over the rim of her cup to them.

"Nothing," they chorused.

"Did you take anything?" little Paul was the first to ask.

"No," she said, then her voice softened for their baby. "I hadn't the time. I'll take you something the next time. I'm going to take you a cowboy outfit."

"What will you get for me?" little Dan asked.

"What are you wanting? An Indian set?"

"No, I would be wanting a cowboy outfit too," he said. "You get real guns with them."

"They're just pretend, pet. But they look real," Grace said. Little Dan made drills in his mashed potatoes with his fork and dreamed he was The Lone Ranger.

"Where's Colin?" Grace asked her mother.

"He's upstairs. Getting ready to go out. Wait till you see the dress of him."

Grace didn't hear the last. "Where's Duncan?" she asked.

"He's been in and out again," her father carried their plates to the sink. "He's courting."

"Duncan?" Grace's head snapped towards her father. "Who's he going with?" she sounded aghast at what she was hearing.

"Well, he has a girl anyway," her father put his head back and opened his mouth in a wide grin.

"That's right, make game," her mother's hackles rose.

"Don't be daft," John Clark wiped the dishcloth across a blue plate. "Who's making game?" he shook his head. "Only a joke," he said, and he closed his mouth.

"Are you staying home?" Colin put his Brylcreamed head around the living room door.

"No," Grace stared at his style. That silver grey suit was new, the trousers were the latest fashion, she didn't know how he got his feet through the bottoms of them. His shirt was like the snow, her mother would have ironed it to perfection. On his feet he wore winkle picker shoes. They were new since last time too.

"You are," he told her. "You're needed," and he closed the door, leaving the smell of his Brylcream with them.

From outside they heard the sound of his car engine firing. Their ears followed his car's sound out of the village.

Marjie studied Grace. She didn't think that Grace would ever come back. She looked at Grace's hooped ears, her hair pinned so neat and tidy that not even one hair hung loose from it. Grace's hair shone like silk. When she thought that no-one would see her, she put her hand up to her own hair. It was so strong and curly that her hand almost bounced from it. She took her hand from her hair and put it into her lap with the other one and bowed her head.

"I took you that two skirts." Marjie looked up and across to Grace's painted mouth. "I never wear them now," Grace said.

"Ta," Marjie turned in on herself and looked down again. The skirt she was wearing was one of Grace's. Grace was a lot bigger than her, but Marjie made it fit.

"Always getting," her mother said. "She can give one to Jeannie."

Marjie didn't speak. One shoe played with the other one. They had once been Grace's also. They were too big for her and she couldn't walk right with their high heels, her ankles buckled sometimes, but if she put cotton wool into the toes they were perfect, she could hang on to them.

"I'm going to do my homework," she said. "It's the exams in two weeks." She could have ripped her tongue from her mouth the minute the words were said.

"Never mind homework. Finish that dishes. Then you can take the brush over this floor," her mother sang the same tune. "Homework! Who do you think you are?" she wouldn't let be.

"I hope you're not using my bed," Grace bent to light her cigarette from the fire.

"No," Marjie said and she hoped her mother would keep her mouth shut on that score. Who'd dare? she thought as she went ben to the kitchen. You'd brain them.

"Are you home for good?" Marjie was awake when Grace came up.

"Don't be daft. What do you think I am?" and she hung her jacket over the back of the chair.

Marjie mouthed the first line of Morte d'Arthur and moved away from Jeannie's feet. She'd never get the hang of it. She'd need a month to know it. She closed her eyes and tried again. '*And all day long the noise of battle rolled, Between the mountains and the dark green sea.*' She opened her eyes and looked at the page. She read the first two lines. Right, she'd got that right. She tried the next two. '*Until King Arthur's table man by man, Had fallen into Lyonesse about their lord, King Arthur.*' She closed her eyes and nothing came through to her. She opened them again. It was no use. She hadn't a clue what she was reading. And who or what was Lyonesse?

"Keep your feet to yourself," she was irritable with Jeannie. She looked at the ceiling and tried it again. '*Until King Arthur's table...*' she looked at the page. Right, that was right. '*Until King Arthur's table...*' That was it. That was all of it. She closed the book and dropped it onto the floor. She'd have to try to learn it on the bus in the morning, where things were quieter.

"What are you doing still waken?" Grace folded her tie and put it on the chair.

"I was trying to learn a poem for tomorrow," Marjie said.

"Well, you can get to sleep. The light's going off when I'm ready."

"Ma's wanting you home," Marjie's head was on the pillow.

"She can want," Grace spoke through a mouthful of hairpins. "When's your exams anyway?"

"In two weeks' time."

"Are you still doing O.K.?"

"Ay, but it's getting harder. It's hard to do my homework. I should be doing more."

"Well, do it. Do it," Grace's eyes flashed at her sister. "It's the only way you're going to get out of here," and she pressed the switch.

"Myself and Margaret are going to try to get into Edinburgh University," Marjie said from the darkness. "We start working for the Highers in August. A year and a bit from now I could be there," the hope was still with her. She put her head beneath the blankets and dreamt on it.

_____

"Read that," her mother thrust the manilla envelope at Grace.

"What is it?" Grace blew smoke rings from her mouth.

"Read it," she heard the urgency in her mother's voice. "Before he comes in."

Grace put her cigarette on the tiled mantelpiece and took the single sheet from the envelope. As she read the typewritten lines her heart sank within her.

"When did this come?" her eyes met her mother's.

"It's the fourth. I burnt the rest. Your father'll go mad when he finds out," her mother twisted her ring around her finger.

"Well, he's going to find out. It says," she looked back to the sheet and read from it, " 'if payment is not forthcoming we shall be forced to repossess the dwelling.' They'll take the house," and Grace put her cigarette back between her lips and handed the letter to her mother.

"Your father thinks we're up to date," her mother pushed the doubled envelope back into her apron pocket.

"What are you going to do?" Grace asked her again.

"I thought I could pay off something without him knowing."

"He'll have to know. You can't hide that," Grace shrugged the problem from her.

"You must have something," her mother said.

"Me? I have nothing. I came home on a warrant."

"You must have something. Don't sit there and tell me you've nothing. You've sent nothing since weeks," her mother's voice was ragged.

"I need what I get," Grace defended herself. "I went away with nothing on my back. All the other girls have such nice things."

"And I need your money too," her mother's tone hardened. "How much have you got?"

"I've nothing. I spend what I get."

"Have you nothing you could sell?"

"What?" Grace wasn't ready for this. "I'm not selling my things."

"Well, we've nothing," her mother ground out.

"What about that car out there?" Grace's voice was becoming wild.

"He can't sell his car. That boy worked hard for what

he's got and to keep the lot of you," there was finality in her mother's words.

"Well, I'm not selling my things," Grace turned from her mother and looked at the wallpaper.

"Your father'll go mad."

Let him, Grace thought and made more rings from her mouth. Let the whole lot go mad. I'm not selling anything and I'm not coming back here to live.

"Why will your father go mad?" No-one heard John Clark coming. He stood in the doorway and looked across to the two of them.

"Nothing. Nothing at all. Standing there and listening to people," Cis was hasty in her defence.

"Do you know that I'm supposed to leave the W.R.A.F.?" Grace turned a flushed face to him.

"That was just your mother talking," he scooped their cat from his chair. "Why would you leave when you like it? All anyone's asking is for you to try and send a little home to us. It would help," he sat in his chair and took his bonnet from his head.

"She's got her bounty. She gets a lump sum when she leaves," Cis said.

"What are you talking about? The lassie can't leave for that," he didn't know what he was hearing. It was a job to follow Cis sometimes.

Grace made a strange sound from her throat and looked back to the wall.

"The lassie can't leave for that," Cis' voice climbed in her mimickry. "Well, the lassie can bloody well leave for that," and she tore the envelope from her pocket and threw it at him.

"What's this?" he sounded stupid in his surprise.

"Read it."

"What's it all about?" he put his fingers into the envelope.

"You'll find out."

"What's it all about?" he still sounded stupified after he read it.

"Are you stupid or something?" Cis was merciless in her fear. "What do you think it's about? They're going to take the house," and there was something that sounded cruelly triumphant in the way she spoke.

"Where did the money go?" his face had collapsed on him.

"Where do you think it went? Keeping the bloody lot of you," she screamed at him.

"But the house money?" he tried to find a way round what was going on in him. "Surely you didn't tamper with that?"

"Well, there is no house money. There's no money anywhere. So she can get herself home," she whirled on Grace.

There was nothing left in him. "What a mess everything always is." He shook his head, his eyes were dull.

"It says there that if we pay something of the arrears they'll give us a bit more time," Cis said.

"And where's the money to come for that?" he had sunk into himself. "I'll see if I can ask someone," and he rose and walked slowly back to the shed. His bonnet was still hanging from his hand.

"I'll sell my camera and my transistor," Grace said. "And you may as well take my coat too. It's new and I've a costume," and she turned back to the wall.

"It'll be alright," her mother spoke easier. "Your

father'll get something," and she bent and picked a hot coal from the hearth and threw it back onto the fire. "If you hurry you'll catch the bus. The things'll go in my bag."

"No," Grace said. "No, I'll go with them in the morning."

"And you can get yourself out of that school," her mother started on Marjie as soon as she walked into the house. "Keeping big ones like you in school. I'll give you school. You can get yourself a bloody job," and she left the marks of her hand on Marjie's face.

"Alright, if that's what you're wanting," Marjie blazed at her mother, and she flung her schoolbag behind her father's chair. "If that's the way you're wanting it, I will."

"I do want it. I do want it. Keeping big buggers on nothing."

"Right then, I will. I'll leave tomorrow. I'm sick of this."

"You're sick of it. You're sick of it," and her mother's hand flew again.

"Are you waken, Grace?" Marjie spoke to the other bed.

"No," Grace answered. "Go to your sleep."

"I'm leaving school tomorrow."

"Don't talk daft," Grace's tone was short. "Get to sleep."

"I am Grace. Honest. I'm fed up with the fighting.

Anyway, she said I had to."

"Don't be more stupid than you can help. She's always saying that. You've been getting it since you went to the Academy. Never mind her."

"No, she means it this time. I'm sixteen now. I should have left last summer. They can't keep me in school. I always knew that."

"Don't be daft," Grace's voice came strange to Marjie.

"Are you crying?"

"No, I'm not crying. Now, will you shut up and get to sleep."

Grace was crying. Crying for her life. She wanted it. She thought that she had it. Away from home she had it. In the South of England she had it. None of them could get her there. There were the letters of course. It was bad again for a while after one came, then inside she settled again. Then the telegram. The words would stay with her forever, just as they had leapt from the paper at her. 'Come home at once. Mother ill.' And when she walked through the door her mother was sitting in her chair eating a bacon sandwich. She didn't look ill, no-one even looked that worried. "I can't stand it. I can't stand it," her heart sobbed to the blankets. In September they were being posted to Tripoli. Anne would go and she would be here. Grace's heart broke at her thought and she put the blanket into her mouth.

Marjie's mind knew a measure of relief now that she faced the reality of leaving school. At sixteen she knew what she looked like, knew the stamp she carried. She

didn't work in the shop any more. When she was
fourteen she couldn't go for a week because she had the
flu'. One of the big boys went behind the counter then
and he was still there, so she wasn't needed. She missed
what her money might have bought her.

The boys and girls in her class were nice and that made
it worse, for she could have been one of them, if she
didn't feel her poverty so much. It held her from them,
made her turn more in on herself in her ridiculous shoes
and droopy skirts. There was still Margaret. Her father
was a mechanic, her mother worked and she had always
known where she was going. Marjie only dreamed it.
Her own father worked hard at everything but there was
still never enough in it. In the darkness of the shared
room, with Grace's sobbing across from her and Jeannie
warm in sleep beside her, Marjie knew she was going
nowhere, and there was no thinking beyond that.

───────────────

"Right, you'll be happy now," Marjie sent her empty bag
sailing behind the chair.

"What are you talking about girl?" her mother lifted
her head from the pages of her magazine.

"Leaving school, that's what. I left. You told me to and
so I did it," and she dumped herself on to the arm of
the settee.

"Now, you can get yourself a job," her mother's head
was bent again.

"Where's everyone, anyway?"

"Grace's down there," her mother made a face.

"My Granny's sick. Rita was waiting for the bus."

Her mother said nothing, but kept on looking or reading.

"I had to get her her ointment. I don't know how she'll get it now."

Her mother said nothing.

"Where's the rest?"

"They're out."

"I'm starving. Is there anything in it?"

Her mother said nothing.

"Don't talk wet girl," her father stopped what he was at and looked at her. "Get yourself into that school in the morning," his tone was brisk.

"I'm not going. I handed in my books. I'm not standing in front of everyone and asking for them back," she put her back against the upright of the door.

"We'll see about that," he said and he carried on working with the needle and the string.

"She won't go back," her mother argued with him as they sat at their supper. "She can get herself out to work."

"Why is she still in school anyway? We all left at fifteen," Colin forked mince into his mouth.

"For all the good any of you are doing," their father said. "There's more going out on you than's coming in."

"I'll not be getting much pay on Friday," Duncan said.

"They'll be taking my tools off. I have to pay for my screwdrivers."

His father's look said plenty to him. He was finished with words.

"He's taking nothing home," Grace said. "No-one says a word about that."

Her father sighed and pushed his full plate from him.

Marjie opened her mouth to speak, then she closed it.

"Shut your mouth," her mother said to her.

"I never said anything," Marjie nearly died when she swallowed a chunk of carrot.

"When's she coming back for good?" Colin looked at Grace and spoke to his mother.

"If everything works out she should be back in a fortnight," his mother told him. "The doctor's giving me a letter for her to take back, saying that I'm very ill and I need my daughter at home. They'll let her out on compassionate grounds. She can get herself off on Saturday."

Grace said nothing and pushed her food around her plate.

"I don't like this," John Clark said. "I don't like any of it. That one should be at her school and Grace should be where she belongs."

"She's looking for a job," her mother looked at Marjie. "There's always plenty in the weekend paper."

———————————

On late Friday afternoon a man knocked on the Clark's door. Cis sent John Clark to answer it.

"Whoever it is, don't take them in," she said, and she put her fingers into her ears.

The man was well dressed in a tweed coat and a trilby hat. He looked at John Clark through gold rimmed spectacles. "Mr Clark?" he asked him.

"That's me," John Clark replied.

"I'm Mr Haynes, the rector of the Academy. Do you think I could come in and speak to yourself and Mrs Clark for a minute?"

John Clark looked at the man. "Actually, the missus isn't keeping too good, you know," he said.

"Oh," there was the sound of surprise in the man's tone. "Well, to get to the point. It's about Marjory. You know that she handed in her books?" he enquired.

"Yes, yes, I believe she did," John Clark said and wished that the fellow would get a move on.

"Tell me, Mr Clark, does she have work to go to?"

"No, not that I know of anyway." What was he about?

"You know, of course Mr Clark, that Marjory is a very bright pupil. Her marks have been consistently high since she began in the Academy. She's University material, Mr Clark."

"Oh, I'll grant you that. She's clever, right enough," and he put his hand to the ache in his hip.

"Now, as I said, I'll come straight to the point. I've come out here to ask you to try and persuade her to come back and finish her work in the school. In August she should begin working towards her Highers."

"She got the prize for French and one for Latin the year before," her father remembered.

"Yes," the rector nodded. "Well, do your best man."

"Oh, I'll try," John Clark said. "But she seems to have

made up her mind."

"Well, as I've said, do your best," and he put his hand up to his hat. "I'll say good day Mr Clark. Tell her what I said," and he turned and walked to his car.

"Good day," John Clark said and he closed the door.

"Anyway, that's it. I'm only saying what the man said to me," John Clark's hands were spread on his knees as he sat in his chair.

"I said I was going to get a job," Marjie's voice was soaring. "As soon as one's in the paper."

"She's getting herself off to work," her mother's voice was adamant.

"You'll do what you'll do whatever," John Clark spoke to both of them. "I'm only repeating what the man said."

"I'm going to get packed for the morning," Grace said. "And I've a shirt to iron."

"Who was at the door?" the smell of whatever Colin had splashed on himself spread before him.

"It was the Academy headmaster," his father answered him.

"He's a rector," Marjie put him right.

"What was he wanting?" Colin stood before the fire and smoothed his hair in the mirror above. "Something about her," he spoke to the glass.

"The man came out here to ask if she would go back to school," his father said.

"Hm. School. It's high time she was at work," Colin said and he did something with the knot on his tie.

"I'm not going back. He needn't bother," Marjie's voice held a mixture of defiance and guilt.

"Anyway, let things be," their father said. "My head's sore with it all."

Colin turned from the mirror. "Someone was at my records," he set his face to them all. "There's a scratch right across 'Lawdy, Miss Claudy'."

"Well, it wasn't me anyway," Marjie was the first one to deny it, the scraik of the needle as it swung across the bakelite still loud in her ears.

"If I find who's touching them, I'll murder them," Colin threatened, and he went out to his car.

"That's two weeks you've sat there," her mother said as Marjie was reading the Reveille at the fire.

"I looked," Marjie defended herself. "It's not my fault that there's nothing in it. You needn't think I'm going to work in a shop."

"Miss High and Mighty. Who do you think you are? Not going to work in a shop indeed. You'll take what you can find my girl. Mind your feet," and her mother caught the dirt beneath Marjie with the brush. "You can damn well get yourself back."

"Eh?" Marjie stopped in the middle of a sentence about 'How to tell if a boy is interested'.

"You heard. Get out of that chair so I can brush under it."

Marjie scrambled from the chair and into another one.

"You're going back," her mother said. "No Family Allowance or nothing coming in."

"I can't go back now. You can't make me. I'm not going. Everyone'll be wondering," she screeched to her mother.

"Let everyone wonder," her mother said. "I don't care. And don't talk like that to me. Who do you think you are?" her mother pushed the chair back with her knee. "You can get yourself on that bus my girl. I'm not having you sitting over me doing nothing. You're father wants you to go back, the man came to the house wanting you back," her mother paused at her brushing and turned to look at Marjie. "You're going," she said, and she waved the brush in front of Marjie's face.

"I'm not and you can't make me. You're not the boss of me," Marjie flared.

"You impudent swine," and she clipped Marjie's ankle with the head of the brush. "You'll do as I say."

"That's what you think," Marjie shouted and she dived for the safety of the open door.

Marjie was waiting for the school bus with the other scholars the following morning. If anyone thought her reappearance among them strange they kept it to themselves, and said nothing to her. On the bus Margaret asked every question and Marjie answered in monosyllables. Margaret was giggly at Marjie's return, and her tongue didn't rest for the entire journey. The rest of her class accepted her return without question, as they tackled their theorems and Shakespeare's plays. She simply told them the truth, that she hadn't been able to find the kind of work she was looking for. The teachers' faces told her they were glad to see her when they handed her books back. They all said the same thing, that she would have to work extra hard to make up for what she missed.

She worked very hard up until the end of the June of that year. She had been back at school for three months and again she took first prize for French and she was third in English. Then everyone handed in their books. That year was over and the summer holidays were about to begin. This time Marjie had a job to go to. Grace and her mother had found it for her in the paper. They said that if they were to wait for her they'd wait forever.

The lady came to see her, they were holidaying nearby. That was why they advertised in a northern newspaper. She was a nice lady, professional, and she said that Marjie seemed to be the kind of girl they were looking for to clean the house and to keep an eye on their two little girls. She was glad that Marjie didn't bite her fingernails, that wouldn't have been a good example to the girls.

She didn't tell them at school that she was going into service. It didn't sound right. Instead she made it sound better. "I'm going to be a children's nurse," she said in reply to their friendly questions. They were pleased for her and said if that was what she was wanted to do. She told them it was, she'd always loved bairns. They wished her good luck and told one another that they'd see each other when they returned.

There wasn't much to go into Marjie's case. Her mother went on the bus and came back with new shoes for her. Grace gave her a handbag and a blouse.

She finished school on the Wednesday. On the Sunday the people came in their big green car for her. Little Paul was the one with the news.

"There's a big car stopped outside," he said. "There's people in it."

"That'll be them, that'll be them," her mother sounded flustered. "Come away from that window," she warned Jeannie. "They'll see you."

"Right," Marjie picked up her case from the floor. Her handbag dangled from her wrist.

"Are you going in that car, Marjie?" little Paul looked at her. Shy with his sister, he put his fingers into his mouth and made strange shapes with it.

"Ay, pet. I'll take you a toy when I come home," she said.

"You better hurry or you'll have them at the door," her mother told her. "Mind the money," and her face was smiling.

"See you," Jeannie touched Marjie's arm. Her eyes were shiny and she didn't sniff.

"See you then," Marjie looked at them. She wanted to be away.

"Give me that," her father had come from the shed. She put her case into his hand.

"I'll send as much as I can," she stopped at the door and promised her mother. Her mother was in her chair.

The man opened the boot of his car and her father put the case into it. Then he opened the back door for her and spoke to the man. "Watch yourself, now," he came back to Marjie and she wouldn't look at him. "Write to us just as soon as you're settled. Your mother'll be worrying."

"I'll send what I can," she promised him, and her eyes were on her new cream shoes.

"I know that," he said. "I know that fine. Just watch yourself, that's all," his eyes were moist and he was struggling with his breath.

"Ay," she said and she climbed into the back seat beside the two little girls.

"Cheerio," Jeannie and the two little ones came to stand with him, to peer through the car's window and to smile and wave.

"Cheerio, then," her father helped her to close the car's door.

The big green car rolled away from them. July was beginning and Marjie was on her way to Edinburgh for good.